COMBO
The July Fourth Disaster: Pt 1

S.B Wormick Jr.

Ascension Comics & Publishing Services

S.B. WORMICK JR.

DEADICATION

I dedicate this book to my parents whom have done more than I could ever repay, my aunts and uncles that have given me advice and support when my parents couldn't, to my cousins whom I have had so much fun with over the past years of my life, to my mentor Mr. Hintze who believed in me even when I didn't believe in myself, and above all God who has giving me the talent and strength to do everything that I will ever do.

CONTENTS

ACKNOWLED- MENTS

I would also like to thank Fiverr.com and the talented freelancers that helped in making this novel a reality. Thanks for creating just an amazing-looking cover. Hope to work together again soon.

Thanks so much

1

HOLD UP?

Eventually, Red's body burst into flames from the electricity. Stephen noticed that Red's eyes had melted away as fire slowly burned from his eye sockets, ears, mouth, and nose. The fire slowly engulfed Red's entire body, but his clothes remained intact. Carl found a bag of flour in the storage room; he ripped it open and rushed back to the burning Red. Carl tilted the bag of flour toward Red and attempted to put out the fire. Strangely enough, the flour just disappeared; vaporized before even getting slightly close to Red. Small embers began to float toward the ceiling from where Red's eyes once were. To Stephen, the embers almost seemed like tears. When Stephen focused back on Red's face, an icy chill went down his spine. Even though Red no longer had eyes, Stephen could feel Red glaring at him.

[Sorry about that. Guess it's a little strange not knowing what's going on. I'll start off a little differently; first I will introduce myself by saying my name is Stephen Wormick, I'm a four-foot-five twelve-year-old boy. Soon you'll understand what was taking place, but let's go back to..... June 28th, 2000 around 11 am where you find me on yet another flight headed to Chicago.]

"Hope my favorite passenger is doing well. Here Stephen... I got you two extra bags. I know how much you love the honey-roasted ones." A flight attendant smiled as she leaned toward Stephen, sitting by the window to hand him three bags of honey-roasted peanuts. A gentleman in the aisle seat slowly lowered his sunglasses, in an attempt to peek down the flight attendant's shirt.

"Thank you, Dawn! Tell Alice I said hi." Stephen reached for the peanuts as he noticed what the gentleman at the end of the aisle was attempting to do.

"You know I will let her know! I'll check on you again before we land. Just let me know if you need anything else." Dawn then continued to push her food cart down the aisle toward the back of the plane so she could assist other passengers.

"I wouldn't if I were you, sir." Stephen sternly suggested, as he opened one bag of peanuts.

The gentleman then removed his glasses and was watching Dawn from behind as she continued down the aisle.

"What's up? You talking to me?" the gentleman asked. "Yea. I can see how you're staring at her and can *only*

imagine what you're thinking. I'm telling you now, it's a waste of your time."

"What could you possibly know?"

"I've been flying back and forth from Detroit to Chicago for the last 5 or 6 years, I don't remember, but Ms. Dawn has been my personal flight assistant for at least 8 of those flights."

"Your point?"

"My point is I know her and whatever you're thinking, Dawn isn't that type of woman. She is happily married, going on nine years and has three pretty cool children."

"Let me guess, she has a daughter named Alice; that's around your age? Which means you only know what I'm thinking because your hoping that Alice will grow up to look like her mother and you're trying to get a head start on possibly becoming part of the family; smart . But you're trying to scold me for exactly what you're doing, young man, let's be real about it." The gentleman glanced at Stephen, waiting for a rebuttal.

"I don't know what you're talking about..." Stephen looked flushed and became mildly frustrated. "Alice is 16 and I'm only 12. We met on a flight about four years ago. We had a pleasant conversation, that's all, we're just friends. I just don't want you to embarrass yourself like countless other men I've seen try. On nearly every flight, at least four different guys try to get her number, ask her to dinner or join some exclusive mile high club and each time she declines or even once she smacked a guy, she's not like that. But go ahead, waste your time I was just trying to help. Besides, you staring at her like a gazelle in the wild isn't polite."

"You're a funny kid. There is no way to truly know how *happy* anyone really is. So you had a few conversations with her over a 2 hour flight for the last few years and you've met one of her kids. Doesn't change the fact you don't know what her husband puts her through, if he appreciates her, if he is truly there for her..."

"True."

"Besides..." the gentleman straighten his shirt and puffed out his chest a bit as Dawn walked back past and smiled at Stephen. "...*She hasn't met me!*" The gentleman softly stated as he waived at Dawn. Dawn pretended to ignore his approach and continued towards the front of the plane.

"Told ya!" Stephen laughed.

"Whatever kid...you only feel that way since you were raised by your mom."

"Huh...I'd you know that?"

"You're respect and talk about this woman, the way you defend her when you have nothing to actually gain from doing so. No man raised you to tell another man to not look at a woman like a piece of meat. That's only something a woman would say."

"Good guess, but every man on this planet can't be the way you suggest or I would be the same way. And I highly doubt I'm the first one to be like this."

"Well, you're not a man yet, so we'll see how you are in time as you grow up. You said you're only twelve. So if in 20 years you still feel this way, I'll be the first to commend you for staying true to yourself, because the world has a way of changing us. It's just a matter of time."

"Yea so I'm young, but I've seen a lot, been through more than most, and I've made many unfortunate mistakes. Which I've learned from, I've made promises to myself that I will never break!"

"Okay so you've broke someone's heart before. And your parents are divorce. Doesn't mean you won't become negatively affected by those things as you get older. The world finds a way to test each of us. The goal is to stay pure when you're young, but many of us fail this goal daily, the challenge is realizing how you're changing and try to be better tomorrow than you were today."

"What?! How could you possibly know that...are you a therapist or something?"

"Yea something like that, but we've landed. It was nice talking to you kid. Hope you enjoy the summer with your dad, maybe I'll be seeing you around. You never know, this summer just might be the beginning of some changes for you that you wouldn't expect." The gentleman smiled at the confused look on Stephen's face as he began to walk down the aisle to exit the plane.

Stephen was stuck, wondering how could the man figure so much out in such a short conversation, Stephen never mention his parents or why he was even on the plane to Chicago. Stephen quickly grabbed his backpack and attempted to stand to question the gentleman.

"Stephen I know you're getting older, but you know I have to walk with you off the plane to your Dad." Dawn reminded Stephen before he could leave without her. "I know you wouldn't want me to get in trouble for not fully assisting you. Next year you'll be old enough to come and go as you please."

"Sorry Dawn, I was just trying to ask…" Stephen looked back toward the people exiting the plane, but the man must have already gotten off, for he was nowhere in sight. "… never mind, I must be jet lagged already. I definitely want to say goodbye, you definitely made these last few years of flying even more enjoyable."

"Oh Stephen, always so sweet. Keep in mind that you helped me on my first day of work. I'll always remember how helpful you were informing me of what to do, when it came to things that training didn't prepare me for. Maybe one day I'll be able to do the same for you."

"When I can afford it, I'll hire you to work on my private jet, then you and your family can fly anywhere for free. If I don't have a business meeting, of course."

Stephen slid into the aisle so Dawn could escort him off
the plane.

"I'm going to hold you to that! Just don't take too long to become that big CEO. I can promise that Alice won't be single forever, wouldn't want you to miss your shot."

"*HUH?!*" Stephen blushed and looked even more flushed than before.

"I'm her mother you think I didn't know, but it's fine with me. Of all the men you've seen try to flirt with me the only one that stood a chance was you." Dawn kissed Stephen on the cheek, Stephen would have passed out if she wasn't holding his shoulders . "I hope my daughter can meet someone like you when that time comes. But there's your father, enjoy your summer. Hopefully, I'll see you soon, but if not I'll be waiting for that phone call about my new exciting job offer. Until then, I have to get some rest. I'm flying to Paris tomorrow and then to Texas a few days after that." Dawn handed Stephen his carry-on duffle bag and waved goodbye as she and a few other flight attendants walked away with their matching airport bags.

2

ARRIVAL

In the waiting area, Stephen's father was approaching from the far back and gave Dawn a hug as he walked passed her. Stephen's father Steve is pretty much identical to Stephen, just a foot taller, increased muscle tone and a lot more facial hair compared to Stephen's thin
shadow line for a mustache.

Stephen has always been proud of his father, though despite his short stature, Steve is very strong and Stephen has always looked up to Steve because of that. Stephen has always prayed to one day be just as strong or even stronger than him, proving, like his father, that size doesn't matter.

Steve served in the Navy for six years, became a Sergeant, was even up for another promotion, but while on leave from the Navy, he became the victim of a hit and run while on his motorcycle.

That accident badly damaged his left leg. Without full use of both of Steve's legs, there was not much Steve could do in the Navy, at the time. Regrettably Steve was medically discharged, although Steve signed his discharge papers, he had no intention of staying out for that long and became determined to find a way back into the Navy.

After some physical therapy, Steve regained full use of his left leg in its new condition. Once he felt strong enough, Steve immediately began trying to re-enlist into the Navy, despite what most doctors told him. He spent the last five years trying to prove that he was strong enough to return, but he was repeatedly rejected and running out of time because of his age.

Steve is extremely friendly and a well-liked man with many talents, but Stephen noticed changes in his father every time he's rejected by the Navy. Over the past few summers, Steve has become more frustrated, easily agitated and less optimistic; he sometimes even seems doubtful at times, and not just about the Navy but even normal day to day enjoyments seem to be less fun for his father as they once were. Losing hope of returning before he turns 39 in December of 2006, at which time he'll be considered too old by military standards, to ever return.

Other than Steve's physical strength, Stephen also looked up to his dad for his athletic ability, before his accident, at nearly every sport. Mostly wrestling and gymnastics, but according to what Stephen was told and a few home movies that Stephen had seen, his dad was like a pro. Talented at flipping, skilled at multiple fighting moves and styles, he can even bench press over 300 pounds. These were things Stephen dreamed he would be able to do one day, he even told his dad that he would be able to lift more than him when he gets older, in hopes to lift his father's spirits. As for now Stephen can barely lift the 45-pound bar, so he has a lot of work to do.

"Munchkin. Munchkin! You alright?" Steve repeated trying to get Stephen's attention.

"I....I....um...I'm..." Still in shock over the kiss on the cheek.

"Stephen! I know she's gorgeous, but you gotta snap out of it or women will walk all over you. Besides she's older than your mother, it'll never happen. But maybe with someone like her one day."

Stephen came to, as the blood began to flow back to his brain. "Hey Dad. Sorry." Stephen said as he gave his father a manly handshake.

"Oh, still too good to give you're old man a hug and a kiss I see, but *Ms. Dawn*, who you've barely even known for maybe a day, can kiss you? Ok it's cool I see how it is, I'm only your father." Steve looked at Stephen while rubbing his uncut hair. "No apologies needed I get it, Ms. Dawn is something special, not sure what you did to get a kiss from her, I know if your mom looked like that we'd probably still be together."

"I don't know if I should be more upset that you ruined a perfect picture in my head or that you kind of insulted my mom."

"You know I loved your mother, just saying I don't think any man could walk away from that!"

"Great, you sound like the guy on the plane that sat next to me."

"What guy?"

"Some guy was looking down Ms. Dawn's shirt and kept staring at her butt. He tried to tell me how I'll be the same way one day. That I only respect women now because I'm being raised by mom in Detroit. Also tried to say how my break-up with Patricia..."

"Again, you and that girl son." Steve and Stephen walked, following the signs to baggage claim, to get Stephen's suitcases.

"It's different this time I really messed up. Took me all year of trying to make up for what I did last year. I did finally convince her to go to the dance with me, but I do really think it's over this time. Especially since mom told me I'm switching schools again for 7th grade. There were a few threats at the school and more fights than the year before, so she wants me to go somewhere that's safer and has better academics." Stephen explained, as the two of them stepped onto an escalator.

"Regardless son, the man you met is right, you know I still love your mother, but you're becoming a young man now and there are things your mom, grandmother, and aunts can't teach you. Remember, you can always come move in with me."

"You know I can't do that. As fun as it might be to stay here in Chicago with you and my cousins. I could never go in front of a judge, in a room filled with people, including my mom. And say that I'd rather stay with you over her, it would crush her to hear me say that. I don't even think I would be able to get the words out."

"Just saying, I always did hope that you would live with me before you go to high school, since it's your choice now. No one's forcing you to stay in Michigan."

"As routine and boring my life can be, I'm used to it now. Just would be nice if I didn't have to live so far away. If only everyone lived in the same state, but I enjoy my life with mom plus I have to try and keep Patricia in my life somehow. If that's even possible." Stephen explained as they reached baggage claim.

"That reminds me, your cousins are waiting for you. You can talk about it with them, I'm sure they'll say the same thing that I said, especially about girls."

"TONIGHT!?".... Stephen coughed, clearing his throat. "They're already at your house?!" Stephen asked, trying not to seem more excited to see his cousins than his father, as Steve approached the conveyor belt.

"*No.* You're going to spend the night over at Big

Daddy and Granny's house tonight." Steve said as he picked up Stephen's suitcase.

"Why can't I just go to your house?"

"Nothing you should worry yourself about. I'll make sure you know when you should come there." Steve answered.

Stephen wondered what his dad and girlfriend could have been arguing about now, did it involve him again?

"Just spend some time with your grandparents for a little while. Stay away from the house and don't even go on Jefferson Street until I say so. Besides, you only come out here to hang out with your cousins *anyway*. It's not like you come here to see *me*. Isn't that right, Munchkin?" Steve said as he grabbed another one of Stephen's suitcases off the conveyor belt, as it came around.

"*NO*, that's not *true*! You're just always at work, so I have to hang out with *somebody*." Stephen said with an unconvincing smile as he grabbed the last suitcase and began to roll them toward the outside doors.

"You can always come to work with me. We can hang out and you'll make about eighty dollars a day," Steve explained. "That way you won't have to ask me for money and can just buy whatever you want this summer."

Stephen just turned his head around as if his dad was crazy, "I'll be honest that is a lot of money that I could have, but I'm not about to work while on vacation. And before you say it, I already know that you had a paper route and cut grass and raked leaves and even shuffled dog crap when you were younger than me. But I have two more years before high school, only four before I'm old enough to get a job, and when I am, I will. Until then I'll come to work two or three times this summer and make that money last all summer, but I'm not going to do it every day. I am supposed to wake up late, ride my bike, eat all the junk food I can and stay up late until August 20th. Then I'm back on a plane home, ready for seventh grade like every other kid on summer break." Stephen explained as they began to walk outside toward the parking garage.

"Ha! Okay, fine. That's a good argument. Don't want to spend your childhood working. You have the rest of your life to do that." Steve laughed a little as they got on the elevator to get to the fourth floor of the parking garage.

"Yea, like you." Stephen laughed, knowing his father hated working two jobs, which only allowed him about six hours of sleep. He didn't mind the lack of sleep; he kind of liked it that way, but he did hate his jobs and civilian life.

"Why did you come out here so late? Didn't you get out of school on June 12th? You should have been here the same day." Steve questioned as they got off the elevator, then walked around to locate Steve's car.

"I thought my mom told you. My aunt Tyra had a combined birthday party for Jordie and Pooka on the 24th, so I promised I would stay longer so I could go to the party. Jordie was happy, but since Pooka only turned three on the 21st, he probably won't even remember that I was there." Stephen explained as they approached Steve's brown 1996 Chevrolet Blazer.

"How old is Jordan?" Steve said as he used the car remote to unlock the doors.

"They're three years apart, so Jordan will be six on July 13th; he might not remember I came, either, but my aunt was happy and I had some fun." Stephen said as he opened the trunk and tossed one suitcase in.

"What's Poopoo's actual name?" Steve asked, putting the other suitcase in the trunk.

"Pooka, you mean, and his actual name is Nathaniel." Stephen had a dumbfounded look on his face as he closed the trunk and walked around the car to open the passenger door.

"Where'd a name like Pooka come from?" Steve questioned as he opened the driver's side door, then sat down and closed the door.

"I don't know. It's just his nickname. I don't ask questions. It's not my nickname. You call me Munchkin and my mom calls me DoBeDo . I never knew why, I just go with it." Stephen explained, throwing the smaller suitcase into the backseat. Stephen then pushed his seat back as he took his backpack off so he could place it on the floor in front of him and shut the door.

Steve placed the key in the ignition and was about to start the car, when he realized what Stephen said and he paused. "Hold up. Now you can get a dictionary and look

up the word Munchkin, and you'll know why I call you
that. But you let your mother call you DoBeDo?" Steve sounded shocked.

"Yea," Stephen replied as if it was no big deal.

"What do you mean, yea? Don't you think that's a little babyish?" Steve asked as he resumed starting the car and then turned around to look out the back window as he backed up the car.

"I'm her only child, her baby. It's fine. I know that I'm about to be a teenager and she'll figure it out, eventually. I hit puberty four years ago, so let her have the little time she has left." Stephen defended his mother as he pulled out a cassette tape labeled "MIXES" and handed it to his father, "Anyway, I made this tape, a little of your old school mixing with our new school beats. Understand that I didn't make it like you make beats; I just recorded it off the radio, don't want you to think I'm lying about making it cause I am not this good."

"You should talk to your mom about that nickname soon, but as for your tape, go ahead and put it in so we can listen. It better be good, those Detroit radio stations don't really know how to make music to me, but we'll see." Steve said as they drove out of garage level four and on to the airport's main road headed for the expressway. Stephen put the tape in the cassette player and began to listen to the many juke mixes that he would listen to every

Friday night on Channel 95.5 back in Detroit, as they got onto expressway I-55 South ramp to St. Louis; which would take them to Harvey, IL within the hour.

[Hi again, allow me to explain a few things while we drive back to Harvey. As one may guess my mom loves to pamper me and baby me, even though she knows I'll be thirteen in March, which is only nine months away. She still likes to think of me as a two or three year old that needs to be watched 24/7. Thanks to my dad 'talking' to her she decided to kind of let me stay at home alone once when I was seven. My aunt Tyra lived on the second floor of the two flat home that my grandmother owns in Detroit, Michigan. So an adult was close by, but still overall I was pretty much alone for about five hours. I did so well alone and my mom realized that she saved a lot of money verses daycare or a baby-sitter. So since then I haven't had anyone watch me, except when my mom moved out of my Granny's house and became a nursing assistant. She would go to work on Friday then not return until late Sunday night. In those cases I had to go back to my Granny's house all weekend and even go to work with my Granny at a medical clinic on Saturday. It was terrible since there was never anything to do. I would take a nap on the medical beds; eat some of the food she had, if it was good. I'd play with some of the medical equipment, checking my heart beat, maybe bring a toy or two and play with them for a while. It was ten times worse than school.

Even though I actually really like school, compared to most kids that I know. Going to my granny's job was fun sometimes when my cousin Jordie would get dropped off at the clinic too. He would be just as bored as me and had said that he would rather have been in school too, which is something I would have never thought Jordie to ever say. Pooka would have gotten dropped off too, but when we first started getting dropped off Pooka hadn't been born yet and once he was born he was way too young to be left in a medical clinic with his granny. She wouldn't have been able to watch him.

When I think about it, Jordie was so young that, chances are, all he did in school was have nap time and watch TV so that still might not be the best example. Anyway that lasted almost every weekend until I turned ten or eleven. I can't remember if it was a year or two years ago, but my mother started letting me stay at home by myself, and even when I did go to my grandmother's house, she stopped taking me to work with her as much so I would have the house to myself all day Saturday or until 4 or 7pm depending on if my aunt Rivie would give my granny a ride home verses taking the bus.

Due to life with my father, every time I returned from summer break, the very next day my mother would be on the phone with my father trying to find out where every scratch, scrape or bruise that I had gotten came from. I remember one year, my grandfather's dog

Sandy bit my leg. Another year I burned my arm a little due to a firecracker, and another year I fell off my bike into the street. My legs got scraped along with my elbows, hands and my head a little too. Good thing she never found out that a car was driving right at me, thanks to Carl who grabbed me by the shirt and pulled me back toward him before my head became splattered across East 146th Street and Vincennes Road.

Then there was the year my dad's girlfriend and my dad moved over one block from the apartment building near the corner of Des Plaines Street to a black and white house on Jefferson Street, some boys had walked over to Union Park with an attitude while me and my cousins where just chilling on the swings goofing off. A teenage boy began untwisting the pegs off my bike stating they were his and accused me of stealing the pegs off his bike. Carl is the fastest of all of us so he ran to my dad's mechanic shop five blocks away and back in less than three minutes. Now, nothing ended up happening, he gave them back then walked off before my dad even showed up, but he definitely wanted to fight and my cousins were ready to do the same, but it would've created bigger problems.

Last year was the worst accident yet. I was speeding on my bike through the alleys leaving my dad's house, going to meet Carl at the Blue House, just a nickname for my grandparents' house since its mostly blue, located on Union Street. I would always meet Carl there before he would be released from summer school classes for the day, which he does every year, not really sure why. I don't think he has to go I think his mom, my aunt Karen, just wants him to stay sharp over the summer. Anyway this time I came flying through the alley and turned the corner onto Union so sharply that my bike slid through a bunch of rocks and some dirt. I fell off my bike and landed on a half-broken glass bottle. My left hand ripped across the top of the bottle and I fell sideways to the ground. I could see my skin hanging on the side of the bottle, and some fell on the inside, I looked at my hand and for a good second I could see my muscles and veins, pieces of dirt, rocks, and glass. Then suddenly blood began to rush out from every corner of my hand. It seemed like my hand was an overflowing pool of blood. I ran down to the Blue House. Thankfully, the Blue House is the third house from the corner so I didn't have too far to run. Leaving my bike on the sidewalk, I bolted down the street to the front door and ran in screaming, trying to keep as much blood as possible from falling to the ground. I woke up my cousin TeVya, who was the only one in the house. When she saw my hand she rushed me into my grandparent's bathroom and tried to calm me down as she turned the sink on. But when I saw her grab a bottle of peroxide, I freaked out, then started running around the house so that she wouldn't get me. I tried my best to escape her, ran out of my grandparents' bedroom down the hall and into the living room where she almost caught me, but we both tripped. I got up then ran up three steps into the dining room and down two more steps back further down in the hallway. I quickly ran into the second bathroom closing the door behind me and locking it thinking I had gotten away. But when I turned around, TeVya was already there; turns out she was just much smarter than me, she had gone into the bathroom after she fell and just stood in the shower waiting for me to try and hide in there. She grabbed me by the hand and began to rinse it under the sink. I was still shaking so much that when she tried to pour a little of the peroxide on my wound, she spilled the bottle. My hand began to sizzle, then white foam formed as the peroxide began to sting my hand from being cleaned. It took everything I had to act tough and not cry until she let me go and I slid to the floor. She wiped my hand with a wet cloth then wrapped it in a white medical bandage.

Yea, life sure is different being with my dad, a lot more stories can be told about the time here than with my mom. Even now, a year later, it feels as if my left hand is deeper than my right as if a few layers of skin never grew back. It's weird just how much seems to happen while I'm here even though it's only for twelve weeks, compared to being with my mom for nine months and it seems like nothing ever happens that's worth really talking about.

When I'm with my mom, every day is the same, weekends mix up the week with no school, but it's the same every weekday. Life with my mom is safe, organized, and well planned ahead; it's a daily routine. I haven't used an alarm clock in three years. My body just knows when to wake up and what to do. There are many days that I wake up, get dressed, maybe eat something, and get on the bus before I realize that any of it happened, like I'm on autopilot or something.

I get tired at the same time every day, and on weekends the time is just altered a little. I wake up a few hours later, causing me to fall asleep a few hours later. Sunday I wake up early for church, causing me to fall asleep earlier that night, then I'm up again ready for school Monday morning then the cycle just repeats, I hardly have rules, because I hardly leave the house when I'm home with my mom.

With my dad it's another ball game, he knows it's the summer and school is the last thing on my mind so he does have just a few simple rules to follow:

1. **Don't leave the house without taking a shower—** that's a given.

2. **Don't leave the house until it's clean and I've eaten breakfast**.

3. **Don't be in the living room when he gets home**, because it's his time to relax.

4. **Dinner time is always at 7pm,** so if no one is home or he's not at home yet, then it's time to go eat something.

5. **Lastly, if I'm still outside around 10pm call,** either to say what time I'll be home or to ask permis-

sion to stay over someone else's house that night, so he knows where I'm at.

There's no *real* curfew or bedtime, and as for planning what to do tomorrow, I've tried, but it never works out the way I've planned. A fight might break out, a new party might start, or Granny might be in a good mood and take my cousins and I to the beach. Life with my dad, or what I like to say, "Life with the Wormick's." is an adventure.

No one can plan how it will go, just know it'll be a lot a fun with maybe an accident or two just randomly thrown in there. In some cases, three bad things might happen on the same day, but another year nothing may go wrong all summer.

Oh well, my tape has stopped and we're getting off the freeway, not much further now. Every year it seems like something changes, I may not know every single street name or landmark, but trust me, if it's within five miles of the Blue House I've been there at least twice on my bike. Can't believe this is the fifth or sixth year that I've been coming out here, that means let me think…three months…times six years…equals….wow that's only 18. Which means I've only spent a year and a half or so with the Wormick family, and yet it feels as if I've known them my whole life, like I've become closer to them than my mother's family. It's as if I've known them longer than I have actually been alive.

Great almost there! Past the Drug Store and fast food chicken restaurant; just make a left turn off East Sibely

Boulevard onto Union Street, third house on the right and welcome to the Blue House. Oh great! There they are chilling on the porch, my OG cousins: Carl, James, and even Lil LaMont. He's a year younger than Jordie, meaning he's only five, he has two sisters. An older sister Keyaira (or Keke) who's six, and one younger sister, Natayshia (or just TayTay) who should be four or turning four, I can't remember her birthday; it may not have past yet. I have so many cousins I can never remember all of their birthdays. Unfortunately, I don't see his sisters though, they must be with TeVya. Well, I think you know enough. You'll learn more as the summer goes on. Now if you'll excuse me, my dad has already gotten out of the car and I'm already more than two weeks late for the start of my summer vacation.]

3

BLUE HOUSE

T he Blue House is a normal two flat, but to four-foot- five Stephen it was huge, nearly a mansion. Unlike his grandmother's house in Detroit which is also large but wider, the Blue House is very tall and skinny, even taller than some of the trees on the street.

Steve's car was parked in front of the house on the street. Two doors stand side by side on the porch, is all to be seen from the outside. The window on the first floor shows the inside of the living room, above that is a window showing the inside of the living room on the 2nd floor. Above the porch is a smaller window that shows the kitchen on the second floor and above the second floor are two smaller windows showing the inside of the attic; a place Stephen had only been to once, and would rather not ever go back, for private reasons from his past. Walking past the sidewalk following the path to the porch, the partly-dying grass lie on both sides of the pathway to the porch. On the left side is a stump from a tree that fell years ago during a thunderstorm. On the right side against the porch is a large bush that's beginning to hide the porch and railing behind it. The pathway and porch had cracks in them and weeds breaking through, while the railings were beginning to rust from age and continue to get more wobbly with every passing year. At the top of the porch are two old 1975 brown doors with the same 1982 black screen doors in front. As Stephen began to walk up, Carl and James stood up to greet Stephen back home for another summer of fun and mischief.

"Wut up, cous'? I was beginning to think you weren't coming this year," Carl said grabbing Stephen's hand and patting him on the back. Steve waved to everyone as he walked past, and went into the bottom part of the two flat.

"Naw just had a few things to take care of before I came out here. Wut up wit you, bro?" Stephen asked as he shook up with James the same way Carl and him had just done.

"Nothin' just waitin' fo' you to get here. You ready to get into some trouble?" James asked with a slick smile on his face.

"Of course, don't we every summer?" Stephen said, sure of himself, as he tried to lean against the rail on the porch, but the rail moved a lot. It seemed to be broken, and no longer attached to the porch. Stephen had to catch his balance from falling.

"No! We end up doing everything while you just be sittin' in the background." James laughed a little, slapping Carl on the chest.

"Well, not this year," Stephen said, letting go of the rail to sit down on the porch next to little LaMont.

"Yea, you say that every year, but we'll see. We got to deprogram you before 4th of July, which is Tuesday, in case you forgot." James said as Steve came back outside.

"Lil LaMont! Is yo' dad upstairs?" Steve asked little LaMont.

"He should be, uncle Stevie." Little LaMont said. Stephen noticed LaMont's normal baby voice was fading in and out; he was trying to act older.

"Wut up wit you?" Stephen asked little LaMont as Steve walked passed them to open the screen door to the upstairs. Steve began knocking on the door and ringing the doorbell.

"Nothin' punk," Lil LaMont said with his arms folded.
He had a little toddler mug shot look on his face.

"Oh, dang, that's wut's up. You just got treated by shorty!" James said as he and Carl laughed as Steve turned around.

"Ay boy! Get yo stuff out of my car and put it in the house before I go back to work." Steve told Stephen as

Uncle LaMont opened the door, letting Steve upstairs. Stephen tapped Lil LaMont on the head, then hopped down the few steps below him and went to get his bags out of the car.

"Ay cuz, I'll help you out. Once we get yo stuff in the house, we can go meet up with Bryan and Red. You know, they was askin' about you," Carl said as he and James jumped off the porch to help Stephen with his bags.

"Wow. I'm shocked Red's not in juvie," Stephen said, opening the trunk.

"Oh no, he went. On the last day of school he destroyed a few bathrooms and was throwing books at teachers," Carl told him while grabbing one suitcase from out of the trunk and closing it after Stephen grabbed the other suitcase.

"Yeah, he should be at the end of the street at Calumet Park. Little LaMont, get over here and get his bag!" James said, while grabbing the small suitcase out of the car and calling Lil' LaMont over to get the backpack out of the front seat.

"A'ight, we can head down there and see what they up to," Stephen said as they walked back toward the house to put his stuff in the living room. The suitcases were in the house and out of the way. By the time they came back outside, Steve had already left, and the summer vacation "officially" had begun. Lil LaMont begged to come along, but because of his age Uncle LaMont told

Lil LaMont he had to stay on the block where he could see him, so he had to stay behind.

4

HIDDEN TRUTH

Carl, James and Stephen walked north down Union St. toward Calumet Blvd. which is three blocks away. On the way, a few guys that knew Carl and James stopped them to say, "Wut up?" Some said the same to Stephen if they already knew him, while others were new friends of Carl and James, so they had to be introduced to Stephen. Less than a minute later, the three of them ran into a group of girls that knew Carl. They asked where he had been earlier that day, even though they all knew that he was in class. A few of them knew James and asked why he hadn't been around as much. Instead of just telling them he moved, he shrugged the girls off, asking why they were in his business and not to be worried about where he had been, but to be glad he was around now. The girls laughed a little; then Carl realized that Stephen was just hanging in the back. Carl introduced Stephen, putting his arm on Stephen's shoulders.

"This is my cool cousin Stephen. Ay when we come to hang out later, y'all better have somebody for him to talk to a'ight!" Carl told the girls then looked at Stephen with his eyebrows raised and hit Stephen on the chest as if to reassure him that everything would work out.

The girls left and Stephen smiled a little, afraid to end up saying something stupid. But overall, he knew that nothing would happen; it never did. They continued down Union St. while more guys and girls continued to stop and talk to them for the next two blocks. Although they had only walked three blocks to get to the park, it took over 30 minutes to get there due to the frequent stops from friends of Carl and James, or girls asking them to hang out.

Once at the park, they could see Red's pure red hair near the slide. He and about four other boys that the three of them couldn't make out were sitting around. Then Carl yelled out as the three of them approached, "Wut up, boy!"

"Trey , wut up wit you fool?" Red yelled back, getting up from the slide and walking over to Carl, James, and Stephen to greet them in the middle of the park. Red slapped Carl's hand, pulling him in for a pat on the back while Carl did the same; he then saw James next to Carl.

"Dang, wut up wit you, fool? You always just show up randomly, don't you?" they shook up as well, and then Red saw Stephen. "Bro! You back!" Red yelled as he hugged Stephen, picking him up off the ground. "Dang you came; these fool's made it sound like you weren't coming!"

"A'ight bro, you can put me down now, you know picking me up ain't all that cool. I don't even hug my family, so you kind of freaking me out right now with the whole hugging thing." Stephen said as Red put him back on the ground and helped Stephen fix his outfit.

"Sorry bro, you just don't know how much you've helped me. I just wish you lived out here. I really be needing some of your advice wit stuff sometimes," Red explained, breathing hard from excitement. "That stuff we talked about when you came here for the New Year seems to be helping." Carl, James and even Stephen were not completely sure what he was talking about, and had a dumbfounded look on their faces.

"Things have gotten bad, but a lot of good things that I didn't think were possible happened too. Like you said, the path to God isn't always easy and the devil will try to block you, but the reward is always greater. It was something like that, but I've been trying to do better. My mom got a better job, we fixed some house problems, and I got four A's in school. I didn't think I could ever do that, and I wouldn't have been able to if it wasn't for you." Red calmed down, realizing that his friend's back near the slide had just seen him hug another guy and knew that didn't look very cool.

"Oh y'all just talking about the Bible, that's wut's up. I thought y'all was talking about something else." Carl was relieved.

"I'm just shocked that not only did Red get four A's, but he can count to four ." James laughed.

"Well, I'm just glad my advice managed to help you stay more positive.   Just please don't hug me anymore. I'm still working on the whole hugging thing," Stephen explained, trying to look cool.

"No problem bro, trust me I won't hug you anytime soon, I've just been so happy. I was going to buy my own Bible this weekend so I can start reading it and learning more. Maybe I can even go to church with you and your dad on Sunday?" Red asked Stephen as Carl and James walked over to the older guys near the slide, who turned out to be their friends too, including Bryan.

"That's not a problem, I know he won't care. Why don't your mom go to her own church or you can even just walk to my dad's house in the morning. He works at the church, so he's always going to go," Stephen explained as they looked back at their friends.

"Yea, I might have to. I've been talking to my mom about going, but she works most Sundays and never feels like going anywhere on Wednesday since she's always so tired. Once her new job starts she said that she'll start going. Until then, I'll go with..." Red paused, looking into the small forest near the park.

"Wut's up?" Stephen wondered, looking toward the trees as well.

"I thought I heard something or saw...." Red tried to look through the trees some more, "Stephen, when you said that things could block my way, you meant literally or metaphorically?" Red asked as he slowly looked away, and back at Stephen.

"No, things can literally come in your way. It could be anything like drugs, grades, a really hot girl that may influence you to do bad things, or even as bad as a death of a loved one. You have to be strong and keep the faith, you just have to pray and try your best to do right unto God. Some things are as clear as day, but other times it might be a bit confusing and you might actually think right is wrong and wrong is right; in some cases by the time you've realized it, you've already failed. It's hard, but you should get through it. It's summer, bro, and we're just kids. We should be having fun. Stop worrying about what bad could happen and focus on the good that will happen. Even the little things count, like waking up to see another day," Stephen said, pointing to his cousin and their friends joking around having fun.

"Yea, I know you're right. It just feels like someone's watching me. I can sense that something is about to happen, something that might be meant to hurt me, and I'm afraid I might make the wrong decision or react the wrong way," Red explained as he looked over to his friends, then put his head down, worried about what might come.

"That's good. Just because you know, shows that you're getting on the right path. God might be trying to
warn or prepare you. This way, when it comes, you won't be shocked and you'll be better prepared for it. Now come on, let's go chill with our friends," Stephen

said, walking toward everyone else by the slide.

Stephen felt that Red was just scared about trying to do the right thing and was sure that everything he was worried about was all in his head; nothing *that* 'bad' could happen could it? They were just kids; but still, why did Red pause when looking in the small forest? Maybe he just saw an animal or something and was probably just being paranoid?

Unaware what Red was trying to look at, Stephen began to hang out with his friends and cousins, but something was happening and going to happen soon. Someone was lurking in the woods located in the distance behind the park, having a conversation with himself, or so it would seem.

"Are you sure he's ready?" a deep, worried voice questioned.

"You dare to question me! I can get another one to do the job if you don't think you can." A deeper and more confident voice echoed in his head. "Don't make a mistake; this is the only window I have. I've spent too much time planning, for you to mess this up, Gaap." The darker voice told Gaap.

"No, I can do it; I just can't see how a child can help us. We have so many people that already work for us that can do this. It's such an important task, why trust such a young child."

"That's why I'm doing this now. Plus, it's not just

about the boy, but his friend as well. He's in the way. On Sunday the boy will go to church for the first time, and if he gets baptized and get saved, I'll be too late. Everything must happen now before he goes to church. Don't let me down. I can only do so much from here; you have the power to bring back his hatred towards everyone, like you made him do at his school. You're pretty much on your own now." The darker voice faded away.

"Don't worry; I will take care of it," Gaap responded to the voice in his head. As Gaap turned around and vanished, Red thought he heard another rustling sound in the trees and looked over, but when he did, he saw nothing. Whatever was there was gone now; Red brushed it off, thinking it was nothing like Stephen had said. If only he really knew.

5

JUNE 30TH

Time was going by fast. One of the older boys realized it was past seven o'clock, and Stephen realized he hadn't eaten yet and had to go. Since they all had different plans, they said their goodbyes and went their separate ways, going off in different directions. One boy lived two blocks away, heading north on Halsted Street. Two other boys ran across Halsted St. heading three blocks west and another boy walked three blocks east, down Calumet Blvd. Carl, James, Red and Stephen along with Bryan who had joined them walked down Union headed back toward the Blue House. The five of them walked past the Blue House and went through the nearby alley to load up on junk food at a gas station at the corner of 147th St. and Halsted and then headed back to the Blue House to chill for the night. They purchased cookies, chips, candy, popcorn, multiple flavors of pop and even some stuff they couldn't make out but would eat, anyway. They paid Mr. Reubar the $97.47 at the counter and laughed at one of the corny jokes he made about all the food they bought as they walked out the gas station.

When they arrived at the Blue House, Big Daddy and Granny weren't there yet, so they grabbed a lot of the bootleg movies from the Master bedroom, took a TV down into the basement so they could watch all the movies and catch up with Stephen to see what had been going on in each other's lives since his last visit. They also wanted to reminisce about things they had done together in the past and plan out something's they would try to get done this summer before Stephen left. They started off with action movies and ended the night off around 4 am watching a very intense horror film. Not the best idea watching the scary movie last, but James wanted to see who would have a nightmare if they watched it last, as if trying to prove they were just too scared to watch it at all.

The next morning started off as just another typical day with very little special about it; Carl had gone to summer school that morning and when he returned around 1:30pm he woke up James, Bryan, Red and Stephen. They washed up, ate, and left the house around 3:00; the four of them hung out for a while at Union park and then walked around a few different blocks with a few people Stephen already knew and some he was just meeting for the first time.

By 7:00pm they had all split up; James went home to get more clothes, Red went to check on his mom, Bryan met up with some friends on Center Ave, Carl went to some girls' house and tried to bring Stephen along, but Stephen used the excuse that he had to eat at seven or he'd get in trouble to get out of it. Although Carl knew he did have to eat, he also knew Stephen was just afraid to hang out with a girl, like he would mess it up and embarrass himself.

"You'll have to sit down and talk to a girl one day cous'." Carl told Stephen as he left to meet up with the girls.

Back at the Blue House, Stephen made a sandwich and decided to go work with his dad in the morning. Planning to get up early, Stephen went to bed early that night planning to make some money the next day.

The next morning, Friday, June 30th, 2000 Stephen got up around a quarter to noon. He threw on some old clothes and began to walk to his dad's job while laughing at a passed out Bryan, Carl, and James on the floor.

"Bet they were mad they didn't get to fight over the couch since I was already on it...I wonder sometimes, how Carl can seem so cool during the day, and then drool so much at night...I forgot he doesn't have class on Fridays...I wonder why Red didn't come back over... Oh, well. I'll ask them about it later," Stephen thought to himself as he walked up the basement steps and out the back door.

Steve only worked a block away, at a car repair and

detail shop on the corner of Des Plaines Street and Sibley. Since Big Daddy and Steve were business partners they owned the car shop together, it had been known as 'The Shop' for short. Stephen had never asked or even thought to read what the real name of the place ever was; no one did. It would always feel like 'The Shop,' so knowing its real name would feel weird to Stephen.

When Stephen arrived, he saw his step-brother was there parking cars. Stephen was a little jealous that his step brother was also 12 years old, but since he lived with Steve he had time to teach Stephen's step brother how to drive. Even though he is taller it still upset Stephen slightly because his step brother was learning so much more from his father than he may ever get the chance to. While getting closer to 'The Shop,' Stephen realized that since he was told not to go on Jefferson Avenue at all and had been in Harvey for almost two days now without ever seeing his step-brother, Stephen wasn't sure if the reason he couldn't go on Jefferson involved his step-brother; maybe he didn't want to see him. Or maybe his mom didn't want to see Stephen, and Steve could have told her that Stephen wasn't going to come this summer. But Stephen did show up and maybe Steve hadn't told her yet that he is here. If his step- brother saw him then told his mom, she would get mad at Steve and he'd get mad at Stephen. With all these thoughts going through Stephen's head he didn't realize that he was just standing near the front door of 'The

Shop'. Before he decided whether to go back to the Blue House or not his step-brother had already seen him. He began to walk toward Stephen calling for him.

"Wut up? You seem nervous," he paused as he approached due to the strange look on Stephen's face. "You must have heard what my mom said. Look I'm sorry, I know we fight now and then, but I didn't know my mom wouldn't allow you in the house, but I'm sure my…I mean your…I mean…I think Steve already worked it out with my mom, so you should be coming over tonight or tomorrow." He explained reassuring Stephen, while trying not to call Steve dad believing it would upset Stephen.

Stephen just nodded as his step-brother hopped in another car to park it. Stephen was shocked yet not surprised about this information yet it still did hurt a bit. True, he didn't really like her, but she didn't know that, did she? What if she did know? How could he just walk in the house and feel welcome like nothing had happened, when it seems something had? Stephen turned around and saw his dad walking out the front door of the Shop. "Well, if you just came to talk I can't son, but if you came to work then grab a broom and sweep inside the garage and parking lot. Then wash those three cars; they have to be done by 2:00pm and its 12:30pm now, so go ahead." Steve saw Stephen nod so he grabbed a time sheet and punched it in the time clock.

"A'ight!" Stephen said, smiling. He realized that

maybe his step-brother was wrong, or even if he was right, he was sure his dad worked it out. Besides, he would be going home in eight weeks anyway, and then the three of them could go back to their normal routine without Stephen being used as an excuse to argue with each other.

Stephen began to do the tasks given to him; he started sweeping the parking lot, the small lobby in the shop and garages. He then washed the three cars and since he finished sooner than expected, Steve told him to wash one more thing: a van. It was one of the biggest vans Stephen had seen. Stephen, being so short, the van looked almost taller than the Shop itself. Stephen didn't even think it would fit in the garage for cleaning as his step-brother drove it in. After working on the grill, filled with what seemed liked thousands of dead bugs, help arrived.

Around 3:15pm, Carl and James ran into the garage from behind the van, asking for a towel and sponge so they could help.

"You two want to help? It's so late you won't get paid much." Stephen questioned why they came, but was glad they did just in time.

"It's...Big Daddy...and Uncle Stevie...they'll...give us enough." Carl said while looking out the garage door every few seconds and trying to calm his breathing down.

"Plus...we need an alibi...so...we were here...all day...

with you cous'. We all came together." James puffed out, trying to catch his breath from running with Carl.

"Wow, really, I don't even want to know this time. It's cool. We got here at 12:30, so you know." Stephen informed James, shocked at what they could have done this time.

"What! You were here at 12:30, PM?" James was amazed at Stephen's response.

"Bro, that might not work, we don't get up that early." Carl said.

"What are y'all talking about? You two always would get up early, if you were going to work. There were a countless number of times were you two would get here before me. Y'all would normally come to work with my dad then be back at the house before I even woke up," Stephen said with a confused look on his face.

"Naw not no mo'. We ain't been outside on a vacation day befo' 2:00pm, since last September." James explained.

"Yea not unless a girl asking me to come out. And that's if shorty is even bad enough to come outside for." Carl added.

"Don't worry about it. You clocked in at 1:30. Little Stevie woke y'all up, but it took you two a little longer to get here, now get to work!" Steve yelled from the back office. They could see Steve manually punching them in with a stamp, instead of using the time clock.

"That's wut's up!" James said, walking toward a table where the towels were.

"Thanks, Uncle Stevie!" Carl yelled back.

"Ok, so I guess we're good then. Whatever y'all was running from never happened? But what about Bryan?" Stephen asked while grabbing a water hose to rinse off the grill of the vehicle.

"When... were we running?" Carl questioned, still slightly out of breath.

"What you talking 'bout bro? Bryan wasn't with us." James looked at Stephen confused.

"*Right?*" Stephen said, and laughed a little, but still confused about Bryan.

An hour later the van was washed, waxed, buffed, shampooed and vacuumed. Carl and James got $30 for helping, while Stephen got $120 and his father said he was going to take him shopping for some more summer clothes, so Stephen had to wait on his dad and couldn't leave. Since James had to go home later on and Carl already made plans, the two of them decided to stay in Harvey and chill while Steve took Stephen to one of the largest flea markets Stephen had ever been to, Thrift-O-Mania.

6

THRIFT-O-MANIA

Thrift-O-Mania wasn't the best place to shop; it was a popular thrift store where many imitations could be purchased. Many items were fake and noticeably fake, some had small imperfections from the real deal, but very few were genuine; you just had to know what to look for and where to go.

Earlier that day Uncle LaMont informed Steve that his son needed a few things as well and asked if he could take Lil LaMont with them. Stephen and Lil LaMont weren't all that close since Lil LaMont is so much younger and always trying to prove how he was just as tough as Carl and James, which Stephen was not. "Be who you are" was how Stephen was raised, until this point, and he believed that fully. If you are smart, be smart yet humble, if you are tough, be tough, but only when necessary and if you're a nerd, then be proud to be one. LaMont to only be 5 was very proud to be a boy, walking with an amount of confidence you would expect from a well-established man, but yet was cocky like nothing could stop him... that was until he got hurt then he would cry like you'd expect from any other child. During the car ride to Thrift-O-Mania, LaMont wouldn't stop asking why Stephen sat a certain way, didn't have nice shoes like their cousins, when he planned to get a haircut, how come he doesn't have a girlfriend yet like himself whom has had one since he turned 3, or just punching him in the arm asking if it hurt.

Stephen felt how he was sitting was fine. Then questioned how anyone is even supposed to sit "cool" or what Lil LaMont's version of sitting cool even was. Stephen has always understood that his mom couldn't afford to buy him similar shoes like his cousins or get his haircut often. He wished his hair was cut, but knew if he had even mentioned it to his dad, whom could afford it, he would most likely ask Uncle LaMont to do it for free, which Stephen couldn't stand. Lil LaMont's question about having a girl made Stephen's mind wonder. Stephen believed he was in love and had already met his wife while just in the 4th grade, her and Stephen already had planned out what college they would go to together, how he would then propose on graduation day during his valedictorian speech, where they would go to get married, move to California, disagree about having 4 or 8 kids, and making a lot of money with his acting career. As of now all of that seemed like what it was, just a distant dream since Stephen hadn't spoken to her since May, unsure if he would ever even see her again after switching to a new school, miles away from Patricia, once he returns home in August. As Stephen attempted to accept this, the pain in his arm grew from Lil LaMont repeatedly punching his arm while he was daydreaming.

"Ha you flinched I know that hurt." Lil LaMont
  laughed
when Stephen's eye twitched on the last punch.

"LaMont cut it out and sit down! You need to hit
him back! Why are you just sitting there?" Steve
asked watching Stephen look out the window trying to ignore what was going on.

"He's 5, a child I'm almost a teenager not only
could I hurt him I'm too old to care, plus I don't hurt
family." Stephen explained in a calm tone, proud
that he wasn't angry or irritated.
Stephen's mom always told him to never lose his
temper or allow others to rattle his spirit or mind,
and never fight or abuse someone, only defend
yourself if your life is in danger especially when it
comes to family.

"Really!? Wow! Who told you that, I didn't
tell you to beat him down just punch him back...
it toughens him up and avoids you looking like
a punk." Steve seemed frustrated and confused at
his son's logic. Steve just glared at Stephen waiting
for a response or reaction that never came as they
pulled up to the gate to enter Thrift-O-Mania. Steve
entered the gate after paying the fee for parking.
Steve pulled into handicap parking and the three of
them all began to load out of the truck.

"Sire. There is a child here, are you seeing this?"
a familiar dark voice whispered from a distance
near an emergency exit of the thrift store.

"No problem...watch them Gaap, you may be able to use this to your advantage, don't waste my time." A darker voice echoed from Gaap's head.

Stephen was walking with his father and cousin toward the entrance but felt an odd sensation. He looked around and thought he saw a strange figure enter through an emergency exit without opening the door while simultaneously changing shape.

"I must be tired." Stephen thought to himself , rubbing his eyes realizing nothing was there.

"Tired already , you've barely done anything all day. How can you be tired. This is why you need to play a sport and stop eating all that crap you eat, then you would have more energy!" Steve responded while holding the doors open for lil LaMont and Stephen to enter the building.

"Was talking to myself . I'm fine dad, I didn't mean I was sleepy or anything, just seeing things." Stephen responded with an irritated tone from hearing the same thing for who knows how many times.

"Well it doesn't change anything. If you were eating right and exercising you'd have more energy which would also help your cognitive function. Doesn't hurt to have better brain function. While I'm thinking about it I have to check out some new knives that were supposed to come in and I'm guessing you don't care to see them.

"No I wouldn't, you're right." Stephen responded

trying not to role his eyes.

"Here is $20, go get you and your cousin some-thing to eat. I will come get you from the food court and we can then get you some more clothes. Watch your cousin, don't leave the food court, and don't lose him, I should be there before you finish eating." Steve instructed while handing Stephen twenty dollars and pointing him in the right direction just to remind him where to go.

"Ok dad, we'll be there."

"Thank you. Love you son, ne'few listen to your

cousin." "OK uncle Steve." Lil LaMont agreed as

he nodded to

Steve, who walked off into the distance toward the Weapons
section of the building.

Lil LaMont and Stephen headed straight toward the middle of the building where the food court is located. The building overall is massive, felt like two super stores put together in Stephen's opin-ion. So many different things could be found, but the one distraction will always be games and game cards. Stephen could see the food court and right across were some very rare legendary cards for two different trading card games Stephen enjoyed.

"See something you like?" the man behind the

counter asked Stephen and Lil' LaMont noticing a holographic 1st edition Japanese dragon card for $1,500. Even more surprising to Stephen, other than the price of the rare card, but in the next glass were all the parts to an even more rare creature from Stephen's most favorite card game. With all five cards on the board at one time, a player would win any match instantly. Stephen could see all five cards in a very rare holographic, Japanese wording, and in protective sleeves for $2,600. Underneath the rare versions were just the cheaper English versions of the cards with no price. They may not look as nice, but they would still give the same result in a card game.

"Wow... you have them." Stephen became amazed, hoping he could afford to buy them all. "How much are they?"

"Just twenty-five dollars." The salesman informed Stephen.

"Really, for all of them!" Stephen knew Lil LaMont had money of his own, which he could get the other $5 from. LaMont could also feed himself as for Stephen eating he couldn't care less about food. Besides with all the cards he would be unstoppable at the game card tournaments back in Michigan where he would win video games, more cards that could be sold, and even $100 so this was really an investment.

"NO...no...no." The man disappointingly responded. "No, what?" Stephen asked, confused. What could the problem be, he wondered.

"It's not $25 for all five, they're $25 each or you can get them all at a discount, which is $100 flat." The sales agent explained, apologetic for the mis-understanding.

"Oh." Stephen was disappointed, yet glad since it wouldn't have been best for him to borrow money from his baby cousin, anyway. "Guess we should get that food." Stephen looked down at his baby cousin, realizing that his responsibility was to his cousin, making sure that he ate some food was the proper thing to do and would honor his father's wishes. Stephen didn't want to disobey and spend the money on something that he wasn't given permission to do, regardless if LaMont had his own money or not.

"What's up? Why you looking at me like that? I'm not buying those cards for you when you just went to work today, you should buy me something ." Lil LaMont questioned somewhat weirded out.

"Need that money for things I might do this week-end. Especially since the shop is closed tomorrow, I wouldn't be able to go back to make more money til Monday, if I even felt like it. But no matter I wasn't about to ask you anyway, I can always come get them before I go home. Let's just go before something else distracts us." Stephen said.

"Nothing distracting me, but these girls. She fine as h..." Lil LaMont said looking over to what appeared to be an 8 year old in a skirt near the food court.

"Hey watch it!" Stephen cut LaMont off before he could finish.

"What? My bad, dang cuz was right you do be trippin'." Lil LaMont said shrugging his shoulder and ignoring Stephen to look at the girl.

"Who said...doesn't matter you shouldn't be talking like that." Stephen said with a stern tone.

"Like you don't." Little Lamont stopped to look at Stephen waiting for him to lie.

"I don't... I've slipped up a few times and didn't like it, I'm proud to say I haven't said a bad word in months."

"But that's not a bad word it's an actual place so

ha." "Well, not how you were about to use it. The

words we

use, clothes we wear, how we choose to act even in private, all effects who we become as humans, as adults, and even more so for us, African-Americans."

"Look I'm 5, not old like you and I'm gon' be cool regardless not a... What's that word you be using... a square, whoever told you that crap sounds like a square."

"Hey, my mom and aunts did!" Stephen defensively stated.

"Well then, they all a square." Lil LaMont said laughing while trying to dodge Stephen who was trying to put him in a headlock.

A man was watching Stephen and Lil LaMont play fighting from an empty booth.

"This is the perfect opportunity." The man said to himself with a small smirk. "You both are right, the man interrupted them playing.

"Huh?" Lil LaMont questioned the man.

"You both are right... your brother understands the meaning of becoming a good man." The man responded.

"My cousin you mean, and he don't know nothing, mister." Lil LaMont laughed, looking at Stephen with a look of pride on his face.

"Apologies lil man." The man said to Lil LaMont while Stephen felt proud to have been right and gotten support from the polite sales agent. "But don't look so proud either young man..." looking at Stephen and waving them over to his booth.

"What do you mean?" Stephen was very confused, shifting his face as if he had no such look upon his face as they approached the sales agent's booth.

"It's important to be a strong, smart, respectable

young man for yourself, your family, your community, and if more people did, then maybe society would become a better place...." The sales agent explained.

"Whatever guy... can we eat now?" Lil LaMont was becoming impatient as his stomach rumbled.

"Hold on now, you were right too lil man, you shouldn't take life so seriously especially right now while you're still just kids. You still should have fun, play, fight, lie, steal, cheat, see what you can get away with. Enjoy the fact that you have no real responsibility or have to suffer any consequences, while you still can. Those unpleasant experiences can also define who you're truly meant to be." The sales agent smirked as he spoke.

"Um, I don't know if I can fully agree with everything you just said, some of that was pretty dark." Stephen responded thinking it was time to just get that food now.

Only depends how you understand it, think about it, see that girl over there.

"Wow, yeah!"

"Now look, I have this chain here. The last one and the charm matches the character on her shirt. Now you could try to get her attention with your intellect and sense of pride. Or you could do something much simpler... " The sales agent pulled out the chain, as his hand became hidden behind the counter.

Stephen believed for a moment that he saw light illuminate from the man's hand, but as quickly as he thought he saw something, the sales agent's hand was already back atop of the glass as he displayed the chain to LaMont and Stephen. "Go ahead and try it on..." the sales agent said, handing the chain to Stephen.

"Wow, looks great! Heavier than I would imagine. Are those genuine diamonds, how much is this anyway?" Stephen asked, hesitant to even try it on, sure that he couldn't afford it. Even if he could afford it, Stephen would rather go get the game cards he was looking at earlier.

"Of course they are genuine diamonds, but never mind the price, just see how it feels..." the sales agent stated eagerly, suggesting that Stephen try it on. As Stephen looked more at the shine and detail of the charm, he finally tried to open the latch so he could put the chain on. "Alright then, that's an excellent choice young man and for just
$500 that's a steal!" the sales agent exclaimed just loudly enough for the young girl that was nearby to overhear and began walking toward Stephen with a smile.

"Cuz it's working, she's coming this way, put it on before she gets over here..." Lil LaMont said cheesing and nudging Stephen whom was still having trouble with the latch, and the salesman seemed to be becoming impatient.

"Alright young man, let me help you out with that. Oh, and it's on the house, yours to keep at no charge. You seem like a nice young man, so I don't mind looking out. I feel you deserve this and that young lady coming over." The sales agent said, reaching out to help Stephen place it around his neck.

"Really, I've never had anything so nice before I can't let you just give it away. I'll work with my dad some more and bring you some cash before the end of the summer." Stephen responded, excited as the pretty girl got closer.

"See, that's what I mean, you are an honest to goodness young man. Still willing to pay me something after I already told you it's free, but I won't take it, this is my gift to you." The sales agent was about to latch it when…

"FWEEETT!"

Stephen popped his head up, recognizing his dad's classic Wormick whistle as the sales agent dropped the chain onto the glass counter.

"Crap, that's my dad… we never ate!" Stephen looked around. Further behind the young girl, Stephen saw his father coming around the side of the food court. Steve was looking around the food court tables, obviously trying to find them.

"Sorry sir, but we have to go!" Stephen said in a

hurry, then looked at Lil' LaMont so they could start walking.

"Oh wait, here…" The salesman placed the chain in a small box and the box in a bag. "…don't forget your gift and remember it's okay to have fun sometimes, don't take everything so seriously."

"Got you…grab that let's go!" Stephen responded to the salesman, while already walking away toward his father, accidently bumping past the young girl that was approaching and instructing Lil LaMont to grab the bag.

"Did you succeed, did it touch his chest?" the same dark voice from the woods echoed in the salesman's head.

"I don't believe so, but you should have seen his face, he'll definitely put it on later." The salesman responded to the voice in his head.

"And if he doesn't, you have a backup plan as well?"

"He will, I have everything under control, and my contingency plan is in place as well. Nothing can go wrong now." Gaap responded more confidently than in the woods.

"YOU BETTER BE RIGHT!!" The other voice faded while Gaap glared in the direction of Lil LaMont and Stephen scaring off the young girl that was in a daze as to what happened.

"What are y'all doing?! Did you eat and what is that?"

Steve began questioning Stephen and Lil LaMont as they approached him.

"NO!" Lil LaMont annoyingly stated since he actually was very hungry. Steve's face slightly became stiff as one could recognize the mild frustration he had with Stephen.

"I did get slightly distracted getting a gift from… *what…*" Stephen defensively began to try and explain turning around to point to the salesman that the two of them were just talking to, yet the man, the booth, and counter where gone.

"Doesn't matter, I told you Stephen! Never mind, it's fine, just get something quick to snack on for Lil' LaMont, I'll just take you to get Taco Bell once we leave. I know that's your favorite thing in the entire world, anyway. But next time just do as I say, please Stephen that's all I ask son." Steve loosened his face, hoping Stephen understood the importance of following direction as the three of them got in line to get Lil LaMont a corn dog from the concession stand.

Stephen turned back to face his father with his head
slightly down, "Um… dad, I am sorry."

"Come on, let's go get your clothes." Stephen said as Lil LaMont received his corn dog. With Stephen being temporally distracted, upset that he was yelled at, Lil LaMont noticed the necklace slightly hanging out of Stephen's pocket and grabbed it, but before LaMont could say anything the three of them headed toward the clothing section of the market filled with a much larger crowd of people, so LaMont just put it in his pocket, which had a zipper so it wouldn't get lost.

Stephen was almost always completely unaware of what size he wore and just like food, Stephen could be extremely picky. Especially with the styles of clothes he likes, since he's more into tech and never really gets a say about what he can wear when at home. His mom just buys what fits him and Stephen never complains, so when given a choice he takes longer to choose than most people. Before long, Steve rushed Stephen as it was getting dark outside, Lil Lamont was hungry again, and the market was about to close.

Steve purchased Stephen about 15 outfits for the price of four name brand. The outfits looked great except for two, which Stephen realized later had the logos on backwards, but Stephen just hoped no one would notice.

7

DAD'S HOUSE

W hen Steve and Stephen arrived back in Harvey, Steve dropped Lil' LaMont off at the Blue House and instructed Stephen to get his luggage from out the house. Steve and Stephen said their goodbye's to Uncle LaMont and Lil LaMont as the two of them headed over to Steve's house on Jefferson Ave. No one was home when they arrived at the black and white house.

The house on Jefferson is slightly wider and much shorter than the Blue House, but since its newly built, there are no cracks, weeds, or damaged railings. Facing the front of the house on the right side is a sidewalk with about eight steps leading up to the porch covered in artificial grass turf, which is to the left side of the sidewalk. The sidewalk continues along the side of the house behind a locked fence which leads to a patio area in the backyard. Through the front door there is a tiny area with one closet door to the left; to the right side is another door that leads into the living room. Past the living room is the dining room; to the left is a small opening and small hallway. In the middle of the small hallway is a bathroom, next to the bathroom is another closet, and at both ends of the small hallway are doors. The door on the left is Stephen's step-brother's room and the door on the right is Steve and Steve's girlfriend's room. Back in the dining room, straight across from the living room and dining room, is the kitchen. In the left-hand corner is a door that can only be locked from the other side. Six steps down, behind the kitchen door, is the back door. To the left are twelve more steps leading into the basement. First door on the left is the laundry room, across from that is the storage room filled with extra food, tools, supplies, and bikes for everyone in the house including Stephen and a few extra bikes for Stephen's cousins to use or one of his stepbrother's friends. Next to the storage room is Steve's private bathroom painted Stephen's favorite dark color, purple; across from Steve's bathroom is Steve's girlfriend's private office. The last door at the end of the hall on the right is the utility room; because of the size, Steve turned it into a weight room. Up the steps and out the back door is the patio area, used for many things such as barbecues, picnics, parties, or just relaxing in lawn chairs under the setting sun. A pathway through the grass leads to a larger parking area where up to three cars can park. It connects to an alley. In the right corner is a small shed colored black and white like the house, and in the left corner a tall tree that gives the parked cars shade from the sun. Other than the parking area, a black metal fence surrounds the house.

Steve and Stephen entered through the back door to turn off the alarm. Stephen quickly went to throw his bags under his step-brother's bed, but his father informed him that the office was turned into a room and that Stephen would have to sleep in the basement this summer. Upset about this new information, Stephen headed into the basement hoping not to run into his step-mom before she got home to avoid uncomfortable tension. Stephen quickly placed his entire luggage under the small twin size bed in the basement, while Steve had grabbed a Pepsi, his favorite drink out the refrigerator and a bag of chips out of the cabinet to relax in the living room on the new futon. Stephen placing the bags of new clothes on the bed, realized lil LaMont still had the chain and hoped he could hurry up and get back to the Blue House before lil LaMont left with Uncle LaMont. Stephen quickly went to get his bike out of the storage room up the basement stairs and out the back door. He heard the doorbell; assuming it was the mailman or someone else for his father, Stephen shut the back door and headed toward the alley with his bike. As Stephen got on his bike to ride off, he suddenly heard the Wormick whistle come from his father at the front door. Stephen knew to go back, but instead of going through the alley, he rode along the side of the house out the fence to see what his father wanted at the front door. Red was sitting on one of the lawn chairs on the front porch.

"Thanks Mr. Steve," Red said as Steve went back into the house and shut the front door.

"Wut up, bro?" Stephen asked as Red came down the porch steps.

"Man, I wanted something from you, but I see you can't get it now. Just take me to the crib and I'll get my bike too." Red said, whispering, while getting on Stephen's back pegs.

"What did you want?" Stephen asked as they began
to
ride down Jefferson.

"I wanted you to get yo dad's gun so I could get these fools that killed my uncle last night. My last living relative is now just my mom. I can't take this s..." Red began to say in anger when Stephen cut him off.

"Hold up, bro, you trying to kill somebody now? Who killed him, how, why?" Stephen's mind filled with questions. Red had just said he was worried about something, but Stephen didn't know how to handle death. So many people had already died in Stephen's family over the past five years that he no longer felt pain as much, not lately anyway.

"I don't know why or care. It was just some fools that lived in his area, burned his house down while he was sleepin'." Red continued. Stephen could feel Red grabbing his shoulders tighter out of anger.

"Calm down, bro. We will sit down and talk about this once we find Carl and James. It'll be ok, I know it must suck right now, but it's not over, you just have to stay calm and think about what to do." Stephen explained as he felt Red's grip slightly loosen.

[Wow. I'm going to fill you in real quick. In case you were wondering how Red got his name, not only from his blood red hair, but from the fact that his initials are in fact R.E.D. yet I've never heard his real name. Now, death sucks and I'm no expert in how to deal with it, but in some cases you just can't deal with it. Red's family being the worst of them all, that I know. And it doesn't just go for death, but bad crap altogether. Red never knew his father, Brutus, who left his mother to sell drugs after he found out she was pregnant. If the money was meant to help Red's mother or to keep for himself, Red never knew. Red's father went to jail when his mother was four months pregnant; two weeks before Red was born, Brutus was killed while in prison, stabbed to death.

Red's father had a hard life as well; Brutus was an only child, and became an orphan when his parents died in a car crash on Brutus's six birthday, leaving Red with no family on his father's side. Plus his father ran away from the orphanage not long after getting his driver's license. Red's mom Tasha lost her parents when Red turned six. They were gunned down during a rival gang drive-by and were caught in the crossfire.

I had tried to help Red out last year in sixth grade when his best friend Ed took some drugs from his older brother to smoke. Ed and Red wanted to try them for the first time, while hanging out at the park. The owners of the drugs thought Ed was his older brother since they look identical to each other. Ed and Red went to the park to smoke the drugs. Ed's brother was supposed to be selling the drugs, not smoking it. Unknowing to Ed and Red, the owners of the drugs were watching them not far away. When Ed and Red split up to go home, the drug owners killed Ed only two blocks away from where they were and Red heard the shot. He tried to run back to help but was too late, Ed was already dead. For a long time Red felt bad, like he should have walked home with Ed. He could have protected Ed or maybe deserved to die with him. He didn't understand why he lived, and Ed didn't when they both were smoking the drugs.

Red's life and even his family history had been horrible. I was glad to help him out last year, but I'm running out of things to say. I'm just unsure of how to help him anymore. His Uncle Allen and mom were always there when he needed them. Now with his Uncle gone he only has his mother left, I can't possibly imagine how he must feel. I wonder if he ever put everything together and really thought about it. Chances are he has, but it's best not to bring it up. He already wants to kill somebody; I wouldn't want him to go farther than that. I have to help him somehow, calm him down, and make him reach for the small light at the end of this dark and troubled tunnel.]

After getting Red's bike and finding Carl, they found out that Uncle James had already come to pick up Lil James and take him home for a few days before the 4th. Carl was tired already from walking home to get his bike, so they decided to just try to relax for a while. They brought a few more snacks that Steve may not have already had in the house and went back over to Jefferson. Stephen's step- mom realized he was there, sleeping in her old office. For whatever reason, she didn't want to be around Stephen or his dad, so to avoid tension her and her son went to her sister's house for the night. Bryan was at the house on Jefferson, sitting on the patio with Steve, helping him barbeque while waiting for his friends to show up. Everyone tried to help Red feel better, but if it came to praying, or anything to do with God, it wasn't working. Red slightly blamed Stephen for telling him to relax and not to worry. Red felt that if he worried and thought more about what he was feeling, maybe he could have stopped it from happening. Red yelled, threw a few things, cried, and soon they all laughed again. Before they went to sleep in the living room, Red asked everyone to not talk about what happened, he said he would talk about it more when he was ready.

8
JULY 1ST

The next morning, July 1st, 2000, was beautiful. The day had a more calming feel over it compared to the day before, it was like a breath of fresh air. Unknown to Red, just because he was sad didn't mean he would get out of doing the chores in the house. Everyone had slept on the living room floor and slowly began to wake up to do their part cleaning the house. Red was the last to wake up as Stephen began to go into the basement.

"Come on. Get up, bro, so you can help! It's another day and the sun is out, the birds are singing, and life might just be better than yesterday!" Stephen called as he walked down the steps. "I know things suck but if you could just help us out real quick before my dad comes back to check- in on us." Stephen explained as he walked back into the living room with a load of clean clothes from out of the laundry room.

"Ay man, I don't even understand why I got to clean.

This ain't my house!" Red said, as Bryan began to fold the clothes.

"I know what happened sucks, this ain't my house either, but we still have to clean. Then we can go out or just chill. Plus it'll take your mind off things for a minute or so." Bryan answered.

"OK man, whatever," Red said and got up off the floor to start folding the towels that were in the load of clean clothes.

"OK, like always I do the living room, Carl does the kitchen, Bryan cleans the upstairs bathroom along with vacuuming my brother's room since we played the game and ate some food in there, so Red..." Stephen began to explain walking toward the closet near the front door to get the vacuum.

"I'm stuck with the basement. Come on, you trippin' cous'..." Red grumbled.

"Look, bro, it'll be quick. Just sweep the laundry room and my dad's bathroom, that's it," Stephen explained.

"Man, a'ight cous', but we going to do whatever I want once we're done," Red demanded.

"You know we can still grab that..." Carl began to say when Stephen turned around, pulling him back a little bit to get his attention.

"Carl!" Stephen turned Carl away and walked toward the dining room so that Red wouldn't hear. "Don't remind him. I know you and James don't take no bull from nobody as y'all like to say, but I'm not about to take my dad's gun and just start riding around on a bike lookin' fo' some grown men," Stephen explained to Carl as Red stopped on the stairs for a moment trying to listen.

"Ha. You scared, fam'?" Carl asked, looking down at Stephen, but got no response. "It's cool, don't worry, I won't say nothing. I doubt Red really wants to use it anyway. I just think he needs to ride around and get some more anger out, that's all, but I wouldn't really load it or even take yo' dad's; it's too risky he might find out. I know some people that would have just gave me one, but don't worry I won't." Carl explained as he walked back into the kitchen to do his job as Red continued into the basement unsure what was going on.

"Wait a minute; you know I vacuum the living room. You're supposed to clean the kitchen." Carl said, shocked that Stephen tried to trick him for once.

"Oh dang, you right cous'. I just forgot all about that, my bad." Stephen said sarcastically, tapping his head as he gave the vacuum to Carl and started cleaning the kitchen.

Stephen's step-brother has a surround sound system connected to his TV that allows it to be heard throughout the entire house including the basement. Bryan turned it on and went to the music channel to listen to some of the latest Rap and Hip-Hop songs. Every five or six songs that would play, an R&B song would come on.

"Ay Stephen!!" Red yelled from downstairs. "Yea bro!" Stephen yelled from the kitchen.

"Ay, bro, the light in the laundry room went out! Where are the extras at?" Red questioned.

"Now, you know that they are in the storage room. Hold on a sec!" Stephen replied. "Bryan, can you go help Red out, I'm not done with the dishes?" Stephen asked Bryan, who was walking out of the bathroom and toward the kitchen. Bryan turned the light switch off then went downstairs to look for extra bulbs and give Red a hand so he could finish cleaning the laundry room.

Soon after, Carl finished with the living room then started talking to Stephen while he finished cleaning the kitchen. A few moments later Bryan came back upstairs to the top of the steps.

Bryan leaned against the door as he explained that it took them so long to change the bulb since it was stuck in the socket. Bryan was now just waiting for Red to let him know when to turn the light switch back on; the switch is behind the door at the top of the stairs, next to the alarm system.

"What time is it, Carl?" Bryan asked.

"It's only 10:30 a.m. That gives us plenty of time to do
other stuff," Carl suggested.

"Good, I was hoping we would finish by now." Stephen said, knowing that his dad would be there around 11am to check-in on the house to make sure we cleaned up.

"Al... ght... t'...s..." Red mumbled something, but because of the music playing so loud it was hard to hear.

"What? You got the light, Red?" Bryan looked at Carl and Stephen to see if they had heard what Red had said, but they just shrugged their shoulders. It confused Bryan as he turned the light switch on.

"*AAAAAHHHHHhhhhhhhhhh...*" Red screeched in agony as if he was dying.

A bright light formed from the basement and got brighter.

"What the? He must be getting electrocuted! Turn the
switch off!" Carl ordered.

The light in the basement grew as a spark flowed up the wires in the house, Bryan turned the light switch off before the spark reached it, but nothing happened. The spark exploded the switch into Bryan's face throwing him hard into the door, then he fell in the kitchen floor next to the stove. Another shock from behind the door swung it forward, crushing Bryan's foot, which was in the door's way. Every electrical item in the house exploded as the light switch melted and fire shot out. The entire house went dark, as if someone or something had turned the sun off. All they could see was the growing light coming from the basement. All they could hear was Red in pain.

Carl and Stephen picked up Bryan whose ankle looked broken and the three of them went down into the laundry room. In the laundry room Red was standing on a chair, being electrocuted, like Carl had said. It appeared Red's hand was stuck to the light socket which paralyzed his arm once Bryan turned the light switch on.

"Oh man, what are we going to do cous'?" Carl asked leaning Bryan against the storage room door.

"Uhm?!" Bryan was confused and in too much pain to
understand what was really happening.

The three of them just stood there watching Red twitch as he continued to get shocked, unable to remove his hand.

[Okay, here's where the story had first started.]

9

IN THE BEGINNING

Eventually Red's body burst into flames from the electricity. Stephen noticed that Red's eyes had melted away as fire slowly burned from his eye sockets, ears, mouth, and nose. The fire slowly engulfed Red's entire body, but his clothes remained intact. Carl found a bag of flour in the storage room; he ripped it open and rushed back to the burning Red. Carl tilted the bag of flour toward Red and attempted to put out the fire. Strangely enough, the flour just disappeared; vaporized before even getting slightly close to Red. Small embers floated toward the ceiling from where Red's eyes once were. To Stephen, the embers almost seemed like tears. When Stephen focused back on Red's face, an icy chill went down his spine. Even though Red no longer had eyes, Stephen could feel Red glaring at him.

Bryan snapped out of it as he struggled to get the fire extinguisher out of the storage room, but as Bryan sprayed it at Red, the chemicals just went around his

body and splattered across the wall and windows behind him. The

fire surrounding him had grown slightly, like a sunspot or spraying lighter fluid on a hot Bar-B-Q grill, pushing them back and destroying the chair Red was standing on. The heat in the basement was increasing as the fire around his body turned a strange dark green. Carl found another fire extinguisher in the weight room, but as Carl got closer to the laundry room, the fire extinguisher melted, burning Carl's hands. He had no choice but to drop it and kick it back down the hall, afraid it would explode.

Confused and somewhat nervous about what to do, Stephen took a deep breath, then turned around and walked into the storage room as far back from Red as possible. Stephen turned back around facing Red, who was just floating in midair, still in pain, and engulfed in green fire. Stephen looked to his left side and noticed something out the window. It looked as if his father and a friend were standing outside, possibly about to come in the house. A tear fell from his face as he said, "I love you, Dad," under his breath. Stephen ran full speed toward Red, nearly hitting Bryan and Carl in the head with his body, when they tried to look in the storage room to see what Stephen was doing. Bryan was having a hard time trying to stand while holding Carl back. The two of them watched as Stephen jumped into the air and pushed Red down from his floating state.

Red fell into the washing machine, causing the door on top to close. The temperature in the basement quickly went back down. Ironically, the light bulb had just now broken and a strange blue light flowed out of the light socket

covering Stephen's body. Stephen's eyes and mouth were closed as the light held him in midair where Red just was. As the light covered Stephen's body, there was an eerie absence of sound. There was no burning noise or debris falling. There wasn't even the sound of breathing, just absolute silence and peace in the basement. Green flames from around Red's body began seeping out of the cracks of the washing machine door, slowly covering the washing machine and dryer. It felt as if time had just stopped for a moment until both the washer and dryer exploded. The explosion sent a rush of sound back to Carl and Bryan's ears, as if their ears had un-popped after getting off of a plane or getting water out of their ears.

The explosion threw Bryan and Carl in two separate angles; Bryan was thrown through the bathroom door and crashed to the floor where the sink once was. Carl was thrown through a wall which went through the bathroom and into a closet in the weight room. The explosion completely destroyed the laundry room, and half of Stephen's new room was gone along with half the storage room, and even the stairs leading to the back door were gone, they were trapped in the basement. Both Carl and Bryan struggled to their feet, Bryan more than Carl; they were both bleeding all over due to multiple cuts and scratches. Carl walked into the bathroom through the hole that was made when he was thrown back. Bryan brushed dust and debris from the sink off his shoulders as he noticed that his back was wet from the sink's pipes that he had fallen on.

"Okay, now what's the plan?" Carl asked Bryan while carrying him to the storage room, hoping he would have an answer, as they looked at Stephen. The washer and dryer were gone and there was no sign of Red.

"How should I know? *Is Red*?" Bryan was studying the area around Stephen while concerned if Red was dead or also just thrown into another part of the laundry room. Bryan noticed that the only thing left in the laundry room was the light socket. "Maybe if we can break the light socket then we can stop this, the light socket seems to be the source to all of this." Bryan responded.

"Okay, that's good. That might work. We just need to throw something at the light socket to try and break it." Carl said looking around the storage room. He walked into a smaller room located in the corner of the storage room. When Carl walked back out into the hall where Bryan was waiting, Carl had a rectangular box in his hands.

"This is all I could find." Carl said, showing Bryan
what he was holding, a brand new set of kitchen knives.

"What, those are Mr. Steve's brand new knives. Are you sure?" Bryan sounded shocked and worried about what Carl was thinking.

"Come on I think my Uncle will care more about Stevie dying than some knives," Carl said with a dumb-founded voice.

"I'm sure of that, but how do you know that you won't hit Stevie?" Bryan questioned Carl's decision.

"Come on, it's like trying to hit the center of a dart game, plus this target is a lot bigger, so how can I miss? Besides there's no sport I'm not good at," Carl said in a confident and slightly cocky way. Carl pulled the knives out the box and placed the holder on the floor, grabbing two knives at a time. He aimed for a moment, then threw the first knife at the socket. A surge of energy came from the socket right before the knife could hit, causing the knife to explode. The surge of blue light grew and began to cover Stephen's body. The surge of light looked like an energy field; Carl thought to himself as the light reminded him of things that he had seen in movies that Stephen watched.

"Crap! It's protecting itself like with the fire extinguisher." Bryan said, disappointed it didn't work.

"Hey, Stephen broke through the last field when he forced his body. Maybe I just have to throw it harder." Carl suggested as he aimed the second knife and threw it harder.

As the knife flew through the air and got closer to the blue energy field, the knife seemed to have changed form, but it didn't matter since the knife went right through the socket. The field around Stephen sparked and twitched a little, like a glitch on a computer screen. It seemed like the energy coming out of the light socket had become weaker, as it began to flow around the knife which was now in the way.

"Wow, I think it's really working!" Bryan said, amazed that Carl had hit the socket and caused a change in the field, which was beginning to expand.

"You're welcome," Carl said with a small smile, glad that he had hit the socket.

"Let me try," Bryan said as he took one knife out of the holder that was on the floor and quickly struggled to throw it at the socket. Since he could hardly stand, he had just tossed the knife, and it blew up like the first one.

"Okay, next time, how about you aim first, and then throw it harder? Try using a heavier knife so it will break through the field since you're having trouble with your foot." Carl said, handing Bryan another.

Bryan used all his strength, focused more on speed than accuracy, "I did it!" Bryan impressed himself since he didn't aim like Carl. The knife Bryan threw pierced the knife Carl had thrown; which created a weird X shape in the socket and another glitch happened as the energy got weaker, trying to flow around the two obstacles in the way.

"Okay, if we each throw two at the same time then maybe it will just stop right now," Bryan suggested.

"Yea, that might just work. The energy won't be able to get through with all those knives blocking it." Carl said, handing two knives to Bryan and grabbing two for himself.

With one knife in each hand, they both threw the four knives right at the light socket. While in the air, the knives changed form exactly like the second one Carl had thrown; even the second one that Bryan had thrown had changed.

Suddenly, the blue light coming out of the light socket had completely stopped and time seemed to have slowed down. Bryan and Carl became excited, believing it was over as the knives flew. Suddenly the light shot back out stronger and brighter than ever. The field around Stephen grew larger and the blue field turned into a sphere which rapidly expanded throughout the basement.

Along with the surge of light, a strange dark purple liquid like substance dripped out of the light socket. The purple liquid dripped onto Stephen's face. Covering his eyes, nose, mouth, it even seemed as if Stephen's skin was changing dark purple as well. As for the knives they had thrown, each had hit the blue sphere, causing the sphere to expand. Bryan felt something was wrong and before he could think, Bryan pushed Carl down the hall then looked back toward the sphere. Carl slipped then slid down the hallway floor right before another explosion happened, destroying more of the basement as Bryan just stood frozen in place.

"Ay, bro? That was close. Thanks for pushing me. Bryan, you good, man?" Carl questioned as he tried to look over Bryan's shoulder.

"Wow that hurt." Bryan said in a small voice as he wiped his mouth and saw blood.

"Bryan!!!" Carl yelled as he noticed that all four knives had stabbed Bryan in the chest. There was a knife in his belly, one in each side of his rib cage and another near his
neck. More blood flowed out of his mouth onto the floor as Bryan's eyes rolled back into his head, and he passed out.

Carl removed the knives out of his chest, but afraid to touch the one in his neck or stomach; everything in the basement was being pulled toward the sphere like a tornado was in the basement. It destroyed anything that touched the sphere; objects were flying past Carl's head and debris from the ceiling flew into the sphere, causing it to grow. Something had flown past and hit Bryan in the head, cutting it open. Carl was trying to protect Bryan the best he could, but when he looked up, a door had ripped off its hinges and smacked Carl's body, throwing him through another wall into the weight room where he fell onto the bench press.

Carl was dizzy and extremely weak as he looked up and noticed that the three hundred fifty pounds of weight were about to fall on him. He managed to roll out of the way before the whole machine collapsed. It took some time, but Carl was able to get to his feet once again.

The field continued to grow; Carl realized that he had cuts, scratches, and scrapes all over him. Carl stumbled out of the weight room and stood at the end of the hall. Carl was out of space. There was only a couple of yards of free basement space left, since the field was now taking up most of the basement. Carl couldn't think of anything else to do. Since Stephen and Bryan were now both inside the sphere, Carl realized the sphere wasn't hurting them. Carl took a step back then jumped into the field, forcing
his body through the field like Stephen had done when he pushed Red. Carl was now in the field and he could feel what he could only imagine was electricity around his body. Carl noticed his body had black (not blue like the field) electricity flowing through his veins; it looked as if electrical oil was flowing in his blood.

Carl continued down the hall till he reached the once laundry room. When, without warning, Bryan pushed Carl down once again; they both fell to the floor near Stephen as another explosion went off. The fire extinguisher, that Carl had kicked down the hall earlier, exploded when it came into contact with the growing blue sphere.

"We should hurry. He might catch on fire," Bryan tried to say as blood leaked from his head, neck and a little more out of his mouth.

"You think?" Carl said as he got off the floor.

It was a little odd. Red was in a lot of pain, but as for Stephen other than the fact that he was turning purple like he was dying, he appeared to be at peace. Carl quickly reacted before something else could happen. Instead of trying to just push Stephen down, he decided to jump up grabbing the socket, in an attempt to just pull it out of the ceiling.

As the socket began to stretch out of the ceiling, a big bolt of lightning went straight into Stephen's head, waking him up as he could feel every bone in his body disintegrate and turn to dust. Bryan managed to lift his head to see what was happening. The wires attached to the light socket began to break as Carl and Stephen fell to the floor with the light socket still in Carl's hand. The electric field began to swirl out of control, while Bryan was stuck staring at the brightest point were the light socket once was.

Suddenly, the field contracted into a small sphere, about the size of a beach ball, covering just the hole where the socket originally was. Then the sphere shot into Bryan's eyes. The three of them were all on the ground, Bryan opened his eyes once more as if he had no choice.

A blinding bright light flowed from Bryan's eyes and

began to cover the entire house. Time seemed to have frozen once more, until the blinding light retracted back into Bryan's eyes; Bryan then passed out as well. Afterwards, there was nothing. Jefferson Avenue became quiet and a calming amount of peace filled the air.

10.1

AFTERMATH

"Oh, crap, my back! Ay, man. What happened?" Carl wondered as he woke up in Stephen's step-brother's room next to Bryan.

"I'm not sure. Where are Stephen and Red, and what about the basement? Is it okay?" Bryan was fretting as he woke.

"How should I know? I just woke up along with you." Carl shrugged, getting up from the floor.

Bryan slowly lifted up off the floor and leaned against the
wall underneath the window as Stephen entered the room.

"Is your body sore like when you exercise too much?" Stephen asked as he struggled to enter his step-brother's room.

"Yeah," they both agreed.

"Are you okay?" Carl asked. "You scared us for a second."

"*A second*...was scared a lot longer than a second!" Bryan was amazed by how Carl was reacting.

"I'm alright, but I'm not sure where Red is." Stephen answered, holding the top of the door.

Stephen felt so weak that he fell to the floor, but Stephen's hand stayed attached to the top of the door, as his arm slowly stretched out, lowering his body to the floor. Stephen was lying flat on the floor, his arm was now about six feet long as his hand remained gripped to the top of the door.

"What the—?" Carl was freaked.

Stephen flipped over to see the problem.

"Oh, God!" Stephen shouted, using his feet to push his body back against his step-brother's bed. Stephen was freaking out and his arm retracted to its normal size once he let go of the door.

Bryan freaked when he then noticed that Stephen and Carl had no scars from the cuts they had received, which caused him to think about the knives. Bryan lifted his shirt to look at his chest; but nothing, there was no sign of him ever being stabbed anywhere and his ankle was fine. Carl was sitting next to Stephen making sure he was ok, concerned about his arm, when he looked up at the cable box and noticed...

"How is that possible? It's only 9:45 a.m." Carl was right. The clock read 9:45 am, so did the TV Guide channel, Stephen's watch, and the clock in the bathroom. The three of them got up and ran to the back door to look in the basement, but all was fine. As the three of them looked downstairs, they then just looked at each other.

"Did all that stuff happen or not?" Stephen wondered.

"Not sure." Bryan said.

"Dare we?" Carl asked, looking at the light switch.

Bryan walked up a few steps and stopped at the light switch. He slowly turned his head to look at Stephen. Stephen paused for a moment, then nodded for Bryan to flip the switch. The three of them flinched when Bryan turned the light switch on. But nothing happened. The light was fine. They were so anxious and worried to see what might happen that they didn't move as they waited for the time to pass.

"Get ready. If anything should happen, it will... now," Stephen said, watching his watch. 10:30 a.m. Came and went. Nothing happened and the light never went out.

"Okay, so where's Red? He's nowhere in the house. Where could he be?" Carl asked.

"Maybe he went home. None of us slept in the spots we woke up in; we woke up in the spots that we normally sleep in. So maybe somehow Red went back home since he hardly spends the night over here." Bryan assumed.

"Well then, let's go find out," Stephen suggested.

Knowing that the light was fine, they worried about what happened to Red. The three of them ran upstairs and put some clothes on. While getting dressed, none of them ever realized that the house was clean, even better than any of them had ever seen before.

Bryan, Carl and Stephen quickly got on their bikes to ride to their friend's house, hoping he would be there.

Unfortunately, what they would find would hurt them; slightly destroy them, for what they would find out happened to Red would be far from the truth. To make matters worse, the truth is much worse than what they would be told. How Red got to where he is now is a mystery, and what he could be planning to do is anybody's guess. Red was currently walking down a very long dark road, approaching a military base in Texas... during the night before.

10.2

RESTRICTED!!!

"Hey, kid, this area is a Restricted United States Government Military facility. How did you get here? You need to turn around and head back to where ever you came from or I will be forced to arrest you!" One of three soldiers patrolling the area standing near two small booths with traffic gates closed demanded. The soldier was holding his rifle to the ground and pointing Red back in the other direction.

Red just continued, walking closer towards them, slowly stepping out of the darkness and into the light, which was coming from two enormous towers. The base is approximately 1,600 square miles with a population of about 6,000. Red is located right outside the most heavily soldiered section of the base, there are approximately twenty-three airplanes, ranging in size and surrounding the area. There are multiple small buildings and aircraft hangers to the left with a large football size field of grass in the center. Across the field there is a much larger building, which is a museum, or so it would seem.

A camera attached to one of the small booths turned to watch what was happening. Red was wearing black boots, khaki pants, and a red hoodie with the hood down covering his face as he walked closer to the soldier demanding him to turn around. The museum was straight ahead across the field. As Red got closer, the soldier raised his rifle toward Red to make Red stop walking. The soldier was unsure, but it looked as if green flames were coming out of Red's hood and floating into the sky.

"Hey kid, are you okay?" the soldier asked Red as he stood there about six feet from the soldier. Red still had his head down. The soldier slowly lifted Red's hood with the end of his rifle.

"OH GOD!" The soldier yelled as Red's face became covered in green flames. Red grabbed the rifle and threw it behind him while putting his head back down. The rifle exploded in the air as Red stretched out his other arm and grabbed the soldier's face.

Flames began to flow up Red's arm from under the hoodie; soon enough Red's hand was covered in green flames burning the soldier's face.

"LET HIM GO NOW!" The other soldiers ordered. The soldier whom Red was still burning began to scream in pain from the green flames. The flames began to enter the soldier's throat until he couldn't scream anymore.

The other soldiers raised their rifles to fire, but before they could pull the trigger, Red's eyes burned brighter. A stream of fire shot from Red's other hand, Red melted the rifles and the lights shining from the towers above. The soldiers in the towers were burned alive and the other soldiers on the ground were burned.

More soldiers heard the commotion, then noticed the lights were out and rushed over to defend the base. Red's hand grew brighter and the soldier he was grabbing turned to dust, as Red killed the soldiers at the gate. More soldiers rushed toward the bright green flames and gunfire they had heard in the distance.

Red became more furious as he shot balls of fire at more soldiers, engulfing them with flames which turned them to ash. Red slapped his hand together and quickly apart, causing a heat wave that flowed through the air across the base, killing everyone that approached. Everyone touched by the wave became ashes.

A few of the other soldiers in the distance realized what was happening. They quickly called over their hand held two way radios the situation then opened fire on Red before he killed them too. The entire base was on high alert, as Red began destroying nearby planes and military vehicles causing extremely loud explosions and gunfire which could be heard for miles. Soldiers from every direction began rushing toward Red, while tower soldiers began to turn on all the lights and face them toward Red.

"RED ALERT, RED ALERT, this is not a drill!" A sergeant rang over the P.A. A loud siren began to ring to inform more soldiers for assistance and warn the population to hide.

"Shoot him, shoot him now!" a Command Sergeant Major commanded his troops as he stood in front of the museum and a large group of soldiers fired toward Red as he walked onto the grass field.

Screams of pain echoed through the base as soldiers yelled out, "Ahhhhh...," "God, why?" and "How is he doing that?" Red continued to shoot fire from his hands. Destroying anything and killing anyone that got in his way. The bullets being fired at him just melted as he continued to walk toward the center of the grass field. Soon reinforcements arrived much more than the base had ever trained for, but because of Red's arrival this was much more than they could have planned. As all the soldiers surrounded Red, he put his hands down, calming the fire burning from his hands. Red dropped to one knee with his head down, using his hood and flames to conceal his face. Green embers continued to flow from the sides of his eyes into the air.

"Hold your fire!" The Sergeant Major yelled as he thought Red was giving up or too weak to go on. "Ready to give up?"

Red smirked after he had a small chuckle and lifted his head ever so slightly.

"I am really not in the mood right now!" Red spoke

for the first time. His voice was so deep and so loud, that every soldier heard him so clearly it was as if he were standing right next to each of them. "Nice job. Good work everyone. You've all tried so hard and have proven none of you will quit. But you also proved that you are all scared, because I did nothing wrong and yet this is how I get treated."

"That is a lie young man, you were warned to turn around and you did not..." the Sergeant Major answered, before being interrupted by Red.

"I could have been hurt, I could have been scared, or even deaf you don't know, your soldier just saw my fire and got scared. *I didn't want to hurt him. So I will give you all one more chance.*" Red lowered his voice to sound more sincere. "Now please, just get out of my way. I might just let you all live. You never asked what I wanted, or why I'm here. I love America, and what it stands for, so just move aside or you can continue to try and stop me. But I promise, that if you do, you will all die a more painful death. Worse than the other soldiers that I've already killed to get this far." Red threatened the defenses in front of the building, as he raised his head more as the fire from his eyes began to simmer even more.

"I was watching the cameras! My soldier tried to talk to you. He wanted to make sure you were okay while staying on guard. But instead you attacked him with no reason, so I say you don't like America and you must be stopped here and now. Now lay flat on the ground and surrender or I promise you will not leave here alive." The Sergeant Major warned Red as his men began to reload their weapons and aim steadily just in case.

Red looked around the field at the many soldiers surrounding him, it was obvious they were preparing for a fight from Red. "Well I guess if that's how you feel I can understand, but before I do you said I had no reason and that's where you are wrong." Red explained as he fell to his other knee.

"And what possibly could my soldier have done, that would cause you to kill him?" The Sergeant Major was in sure disbelieve that one of his men could have done anything wrong.

"He used the barrel of his rifle to touch my favorite hoodie..." Red stated as he lifted one knee. He was back to a kneeling position. Hundreds of clicks could be heard from weapons being reloaded or switch from single shot to burst shot. "...and then he stuck the barrel of his rifle, in my FACE!" Red shouted as he pushed off his leg doing a back flip into the air. While in the air Red threw a ball of fire toward the Sergeant.

A few soldiers managed to push the Sergeant Major out of the way. The ball of fire broke through the doors to the museum, then burned through the elevator doors and shot down the elevator shaft as if it had a mind of its own. Glass from the doors and windows of the museum flew through the air. Injuring many of the soldiers standing in front of it, including one of the soldiers that knock the Sergeant Major out of the way. Red landed to his feet with his head completely down as he smiled and began to slowly reach for his hood.

"Now you will all die!" Red bellowed as he looked up with intense eyes of fire, removing his hood in the process to show that his whole head was engulfed in fire.

"I don't think so! OPEN FIRE!!" the Command Sergeant Major ordered his soldiers, as he began to help the wounded men get into the museum. All the defenses began to fire toward the center of the large grass field. Grenades went off simultaneously, along with a few small rockets. One of the rockets landed a direct hit on Red, the air suddenly became very cold.

A cloud of fog formed around the center of the field and the sound of freezing could be heard. The Command Sergeant Major laughed as he told the soldiers, "Cease fire!" and everyone stopped firing simultaneously.

The Command Sergeant Major was pleased at what the liquid hydrogen missile had done. The Sergeant Major chuckled again as the fog thickened, all that could slightly be seen is a freezing silhouette, shaped like Red. All the troops began to cheer proudly that they had succeeded in stopping the threat.

Through the cheers, everyone heard strange sounds coming from the center of the fog. The Command Sergeant Major slowly walked through his soldiers onto the field. As he approached the silhouette, the fog was making it hard to see and the Sergeant Major had to fan the fog out of his face, to get a better look at the frozen Red.

Once he was only a few feet away, unexpectedly, a hand reached out of the smoke and grabbed his arm. The skin on his arm burned in the most painful way as dark green flames cracked his skin with the pain increasing as it spread up his arm. The Command Sergeant Major struggled, trying to get the hand off of his arm, but the hand felt hotter than lava, making it unbearable to hold. As the pain spread to the Command Sergeant Major's chest, he heard another noise from in front of him. The Sergeant Major looked up at the frozen stasis that Red was in, when suddenly Red opened his eyes.

The green flames grew darker as Red broke free while laughing and flames escaped from his mouth. The pain in the Command Sergeant Major's arm continued to spread, covering his body even after Red let him go. He struggled to walk back toward the rest of his troops, but just before he could reach the closest soldier, he fell. Once the Sergeant Major's face hit the ground, there was a strong vibration throughout the ground. Soon after, an explosion happened as if a grenade had fallen.

The fog had grown and became warm as debris fell, then all remaining troops opened fire toward the center of the field. Green blasts of fire shot out the center of the fog, melting every weapon. Red's laugh echoed throughout the field as he became a swirl of fire spinning in the center of the field. The troops became afraid, as Red gradually increased in speed, causing the fog to turn green.

Slowly, the green dust and fire took shape, a swirling dark green fire twister formed onto the field making it impossible to know where inside the blaze Red was. As the soldiers continued to shoot the twister, the ground quaked once more.

The troops soon realized there was nothing else to do as the twister grew larger. The troops retreated, but most were not fast enough to escape the flames. A dark green cloud covered everyone and everything within the small section of the base, slowly dissolving everything it came into contact with, like steam filled with acid.

The twister became very large and bright, anyone within miles could see. Planes in the sky could see the swirl as it stretched toward the air. Back on the ground, screams filled the air from people being burned by the flames, or dissolved by the steam. Eventually strange smells filled the air.

The ground quaked once again and from the center of the twister, a blaze of fire shot from underneath the field becoming part of the twister.

Below the grass field was a secret base. The ball of fire that Red had thrown earlier killed all the government personnel and soldiers that were down below, leaving nothing behind but three large missiles. The twister contracted, then dropped into the large chasm in the ground. The twister split into three, each small twister then surrounded each missile.

Red looked down into the hole. Within a matter of seconds the three twisters had contracted until they disappeared along with the missiles.

Red looked around the field. Many of the bodies that lay upon the ground were still sizzling, burning through the bones of the dead as more soldiers, trucks, and planes could be seen in all directions. Coming toward the devastation, Red was pleased and ready to fight some more, but it was time to go. He got what he came for.

"My friends and all of Chicago will pay for the pain they caused me!!!!!!!" Red shouted as he began to summon all his energy, flames spread across his entire body as it became as dark as night and then....BOOM!

All of his built-up energy was released destroying everything within a half-mile.

Red shot into the sky, flying backwards so he could marvel at what he was now capable of. While not paying attention to his trajectory and speed, Red heard more screams in the air. As he turned around, he realized he was flying straight towards a commercial plane with 368 people aboard. Unable to avoid the plane, Red phased through the plane, and energy from his body covered the plane.

"Oh no!" "Watch out!" "What the?" Red heard as he passed through the plane and a few people saw him. His energy completely covered everyone on the plane, and just as quickly as he passed into the plane, he passed right through back into the night sky. He then took off, leaving everyone on the plane spooked, but overall completely ok.

On the ground, thousands were killed and many more were injured in the catastrophic explosion that left the town dark, quiet, and troubled by what just happened. Those not injured, were left terrified of the idea that this was just the beginning, the beginning of something much worse to come!

[I can't believe Red would do such a thing, why would he do this and what could he be planning? I wonder who was in the forest watching us at the Park. What really happened in the basement, and what did it do to us? How was Red able to do any of those things, how did he even get to Texas in the first place? I will have to pray about all of this to answer these questions and any of the many more that might exist. Until then you have to wait awhile and read book #2, Combo: July 4th Disaster–Part 2. Coming Soon, thanks and God Bless.]

LETTER FROM
THE AUTHOR

Most of my real life is in the story, but just to give you a bit more information about me.

Wow, I can't believe it's already been 15 years since I first published Combo, back in July 2005. It's also been over 20 years since I was first published during 6th grade. I am now 32 and am rewriting my novels with a bit more depth than I was originally capable of. I believe this 15th anniversary edition of Combo: book 1 is my favorite. 12-year-old me would be amazed and proud of how far we have come. The original 2005 publication will always be dear to my heart, and one of my greatest achievements. Especially since I was still in high school. But since then I've grown a lot, plus that original copy of Combo can no longer be printed, since the company that I originally self-published through went out of business, it was time to start over. This is technically the 3rd edition of Combo book 1, but the 2nd edition wasn't printed to my expectations, so this would be the only copy I would recommend to read, unless you become a genuine fan and just want an older copy.

As an only child that moved a lot, it was important for me to find a hobby. Something I could do alone when bored or upset about leaving friends behind again. So in 1998 I began to write, which I quickly fell in love with.

Unknown to me, at the time, I was writing more than most high school students. By the end of fifth grade, I had already written 37 short stories (one of them being Combo) and one novel that was nearly 100 pages. In sixth grade, I wrote a poem titled "Life", which won me an award. I was the only student in my school district for Mt. Clemens, MI that won.

By 8th grade, I was informed about my mother's miscarriages. This news caused me to become a bit lonely; I began to feel like I would never have a sibling and would always be alone. I began to write in a journal to help better express myself, which only drove my passion and creativity to new levels.

As time passed, I entered the fourth school in only three years, which was L'Anse Creuse High School–North. By this time my father had two more boys, one six years younger than me and another thirteen years younger than me.

Finally, I had siblings like I always wanted. Problem is, my brothers and I all lived with our mother's. So my 1st brother lived over a thousand miles away in Mississippi, my 2nd brother lived with my dad in Chicago. I would only get to see them in the summer.

Soon after my 2nd brother was born, I turned 14. I was finally old enough to get a job, which was easy back in 2002, yet by getting a job, this caused me to visit Chicago even less. So seeing my brothers didn't happen much, they soon began to feel more like strangers than family at times. Yet God does work in mysterious ways; about five months before my 16th birthday on October 13th, 2003 my mother kept a very old promise to me and had a child she named Abraham; my 3rd brother, whom I would see every day and help my mom take care of. But being 15, I felt more like a teenage father than a big brother. This caused me to become even more mature than most of my peers.

I've made many friends and met many different types of people in my life, but no matter what, I've never stopped mentioning my love for God, passion for Video Games, Entertainment, Electronics and all things Superheroes, especially Combo.

After high school I joined the Army National Guard due to what happened on 9/11/2001, as well as pay for college, and the unique opportunity to spend more time in my home town of Chicago, IL, with the family I didn't get as much time with growing up.

After 8 long years of difficult times living in Chicago and many bad choices, I felt it was time to truly dive further into my pursuit of fulfilling my dreams. To do this, I felt it was time to move on, do things a bit differently and try to reach my goals while living somewhere new, so I moved to Florida.

Like most, I've made many mistakes and learned from them, Combo is the beginning of a series that will hopefully not only entertain fans to come, but shed light on things that we all face every day and help find a better way to deal with those difficult times. Especially today when dealing with war, job loss, and the overwhelming quarantine due to Covid-19.

I thank all of those that read my first book. I hope you look forward to the continuation of this series, as well as the many other series to come.

With trust in God, true passion, and motivation, anything is possible!

Thank you and God Bless.